12 Authors 12 Stories

Pinecone Turkey aims to create and distribute art in multiple mediums. We celebrate the process of creation, highlight the creators,
and hope to inspire others to create and share their own work.
Pinecone Turkey reminds us that life is EXTRAORDINARY, and we
should treat it as such.

Pinecone Turkey
Atlanta, Georgia
www.pineconeturkey.com

12 AUTHORS
STORIES
2018

PINECONE
TURKEY

Edited by

Michael Henry Harris
Samantha Thomson LoCoco

CONTENTS

THE WHY, THE HOW, AND THE WHAT

When I asked eleven other writers to pick a month and create a short story inspired by it, the overwhelming emotions I experienced were fear and curiosity. Fear because I'd never attempted a project like this. Curiosity because I yearned to see how the writers would respond.

I think of this project as an experiment, as I do most of my life. Would Benji's interpretation of February mirror my own? What would inspire Virginia about November? Would another writer incorporate the feeling of renewal I experience each September, even though it's been many Septembers since I started a new school year? Why did each author pick their particular month?

That's the fun.

The results of this experiment surpassed my expectations. The stories in this anthology run the gamut of emotions and across many genres: danger, joy, reverence, and loss; romance, action, horror, and more. This collection contains extraordinary glimpses into humanity. Not only within the narratives themselves but also within the minds of the writers.

There are several different ways to read this book. You could read it cover to cover, from start to finish, as you would any other book. You could read your favorite months first, or read them one month at a time, January in January, February in February, taking a year to absorb the twelve stories. You could look at the back cover and pick a story based on a brief introduction of it. There's no wrong way.

Whatever method you choose, I invite you to comment on Pinecone Turkey's Blog or Facebook page about your reactions to each story and the month that inspired it. I also encourage you to read the Contributors' Notes at the end of the collection for insights into the writers' methodologies and the inspirations that spawned these stories.

I, along with the other contributors, thank you for buying this experiment.

We made this together. Enjoy.

Michael Henry Harris
Publisher
Pinecone Turkey

ABOUT PINECONE TURKEY

"Art washes away from the soul the dust of everyday life."

Although this quote has had at least two attributions over the years (most famously to Picasso), the sentiment remains the same no matter who said it first.

It is part of why Pinecone Turkey exists.

We aim:

- to distribute art in multiple mediums, offering various opportunities for the many
- soul-washings we so desperately need;
- to create art;
- to celebrate the action and process of creation;
- to highlight the creators;
- and, to inspire others to do likewise.

Pinecone Turkey reminds us that life is **EXTRAORDINARY** and we should treat it as such.

GO FORTH. CREATE. SHARE.

January

THE OPEN GATES

Virginia Watson

J anus trudges along a well-worn path on the wooded Janiculum ridge, on a mission for the first time in ages. It feels good. His blood pumps and his breath mists in the cold night air, temporarily lifting his mental fog. Tonight, he seeks an old friend, older in fact than himself; a friend who seems to have escaped the lassitude and defeat he feels from experiencing the world for far too long.

Through the pine branches, Janus spies Saturn lounging on the crumbling steps of what was once Saturn's shrine. That Saturn would have a memorial here is something Janus has resented for a very long time. Saturn had not been the one to found Janiculum, Janus had. Janus had been the one to introduce civilization here, not Saturn. Still, Janus thinks, this is one of the loveliest spots on the ridge, or the loveliest even in all of Rome.

Janus sighs as Saturn smiles, undoubtedly enjoying his perch where he surveys the Saturnalia festivities underway in the Trastevere district below. The sounds of merriment float up to the ridge and shouts of *"Io!"* ring clearly as the revelers greet one another and celebrate the winter solstice.

Using his cane as a lever, Janus heaves himself up from the wooded path and onto the grassy clearing. Now he can see down the vale, all the way to the Tiber. The district below glows with candles, torches, and strings of electric bulbs. The lights, a tradition meant to dispel the darkness and herald the rebirth of the world, signifies what used to be Janus's favorite time when people were full of hope and possibilities just before the start of the new year. Staring into the lights, Janus thinks the tradition seems hollow and meaningless to him now.

Along with the dread of yet another year of life, with the month named after him a mere two weeks away, Janus feels despondent. He shakes his head to dispel these webs. After all, he arrives with a plan that could finally bring him what he so desperately desires: an end.

"*Salve*, Janus! *Quid agis?* How are you doing, my brother!" Saturn booms, as he rises easily and descends the steps. Janus wonders how the old man can still be so nimble, but, of course, he is not a man. He is a god, an immortal. Janus, unfortunately, shares this fate of being unable to die. He harbors not even an ounce of Saturn's remaining interest in the world below. For Janus's plan to work, it is imperative that Saturn not be aware of the desolation Janus is feeling. The old god would certainly try to change his mind. Janus rotates his neck, tucking away his hind-sighted face and rousing his fore-sighted face.

"*Ave*, Saturn! *Si vales bene est, ego valeo* - if you are well, it is good, I am well." Saturn envelops Janus in an embrace.

"I have not seen you in many years, Janus. What brings you here on this night? Come to see your beloved humans in all their great cheer?"

"No, old friend," says Janus, considering Saturn's words. Had these foolish and insipid humans once been beloved to him? He shifts his tone to one of concern to engage Saturn in his worry. "There is a scene playing out below that greatly disturbs me. The mortals make a mockery of our traditions for their own greed and pursue such a shallow course of action that I wish to enlist your help to stop it."

Saturn guffaws, slapping Janus's shoulder. "Don't the mortals always plunge themselves into cavalier merriment during my Saturnalia festivities? Is it not the same every December?"

Precisely the statement Janus expects from Saturn, he offers his prepared response: "Their gaming and feasting and role reversals are not of which I speak. I draw your attention to the city center, wherein the seat of commerce a campaign is underway that misrepresents me. Me! Janus! After all these years of comfortable anonymity, these panderers of insatiable desire do feel they can use my likeness to sell their wares!"

Saturn holds Janus at arm's length, squinting at his face for a moment. "Why do you care if the mortals exhaust themselves, chasing objects that will grant a modicum of status?" Janus waits for what he is sure will come next. "But let their futility entertain us," says Saturn, lacing an arm around Janus's shoulders. "Show me the scene."

The Piazza Navona swells with revelers, eating and drinking, dancing and shopping. Festive holiday lights outline the baroque architecture, wreaths hang on lampposts in the cobblestone square, and twinkling garlands drape each of the fountains. An ethereal mist surrounds the statues in the Fountain of the Four Rivers at one end and the Fountain of Neptune at the other as if they spouted water siphoned up from the Earth's core. Boutiques and stalls along the perimeter of the square, all lit with sparkling Christmas decorations, remain open for commerce, despite the late hour.

As Janus gazes upon the Piazza's Fountain of the Four Rivers, he ponders how other gods evaded their immortality. He thinks of Volturnus, once the god of fountains, who had a river named after him in Campania. Certainly having such a proxy wasn't enough to release a god from their everlasting life. After all,

Janus had a month of the year named after him. And what of Sterquilinus, thinks Janus, once the god of fertilizer? Perhaps when human-made equivalents usurp a god's realm, they can be set free? Or maybe when a deity can foist their realm elsewhere, they can be freed? Angitis, the goddess of snakes, had done just so to Medusa, as did Clementia, the goddess of forgiveness and mercy, to the man-god of the Christians. Janus shakes his head. His idea would have to work. Breaking his curse would emancipate him. He was certain of it.

Janus and Saturn, dressed in expensive Italian suits, stand amid the raucous crowd. Janus leans on his cane as he and Saturn look up at one of the large banners strewn around the marketplace.

"Not a bad likeness of you, Janus!" shouts Saturn, out of mirth or just to be heard over the loud music, Janus can't tell. "You didn't look that manly thousands of years ago when you actually *were* a man!"

Saturn's laughter trails off as he reads the slogan under the picture: "Janus Primus, father of all gods." Saturn's face is quizzical, and he turns to his friend, but Janus hobbles toward the next banner.

Unlike the last image showing a chiseled and regally handsome Roman god, this depiction shows an opulent men's wristwatch, the face of which appears to be an ancient golden coin. As the banner waves in the breeze, the coin alternately shows Janus's forward face, and then his backward face. The slogan reads: "Janus Primus, father of all watches," and in smaller text below, "For the man who sees the past and creates the future."

"Look at this one!" Janus calls to Saturn from across the plaza.

As Saturn makes his way over to his friend, he helps himself to a glass of champagne, offered on a gold tray carried by a woman painted from head to toe in glittery silver paint. Janus notices that the watchmaker's logo adorns the front of the woman's semi-translucent white toga and is also etched onto the plastic champagne flutes.

Saturn reaches Janus and gazes up at an artistic rendering of an ancient temple in the Roman Forum. The perspective shows two arched gateways, one in the foreground and one in the background. Both gateways are open and in between the gates is a towering statue of the two-faced gatekeeper god himself. The god of doorways, the god of beginnings, the god of transitions: Janus.

The distinctive pediment and entablature in the image signify the structure as the Temple of Janus, one of many sites Roman guides point out to tourists. Those visitors don't see a statue in the temple, but archeologists and historians claim one existed a long time ago. The real temple is not far from where the two immortals now stand. It is currently a derelict crumbling edifice.

In the artistic rendering on the banner, the statue wears a gold watch, with powerful legs spread wide and arms akimbo. The slogan reads: "Janus Primus, boundary-spanner. For the man who straddles yesterday and tomorrow, and who owns today."

Janus's eyes rove over the chiseled muscles and jawline of his likeness. The artist aptly depicted what his statue looked like before it disintegrated and turned to dust. Janus turns away from the banner. He is forlorn. Seeing the temple like this reminds him of the power he once felt.

Janus leads Saturn past the Café Domiziano, named after emperor Domitian, who built the stadium that sits six meters below the street level. Although referred to as a square, the Piazza Navona actually traces the elliptical shape of the ancient structure that once held 30,000 spectators of Greek-style athletic games. Veering slightly onto Corsia Agonale, Janus and Saturn pause at a large shop window, where the Janus Primus watches are elegantly displayed. A large bowl sitting on its edge engulfs the entire window. Lighting makes the watches sparkle as they float against the deep blue velvet background of the bowl. As the gods look on, the lighting changes and a Renaissance-style painting now lines the bowl.

"Is that *The Rape of the Sabine Women*?" Saturn leans toward the window.

Janus grits his teeth. "No. The mortals have distorted the painting. Watch. See what happens."

As they stare at the painting, its foreground begins to move. Against the static backdrop of ancient Roman temples and fat white clouds emitting rays of sunlight, muscled men on horseback bend from their saddles and scoop up bare-breasted women in flowing togas, while foot soldiers in full Roman regalia clash swords with adversaries. The background of the painting begins to move as well, offering a dizzying panoramic view of the scene. Zooming in on one of the large city gates, more adversaries advance to breach the perimeter. Suddenly there is Janus in the painting, come to save the day. The god raises his hands to the sky, and the ground shakes. The men outside the gate lose their balance. A spring of cold water bubbles, turns steaming hot, volcanically erupts, and kills the would-be attackers.

The moving vista continues: all the beautiful women rejoice, and all the handsome men thrust their swords skyward in honor of the god who saved the nascent city. Words appear: "Janus Primus: protector, conqueror, defender." The view pans upward and comes to a stop, focusing on the serene, twinkling stars in the sky. The painting fades, and the sparkling watches return, floating against their indigo backdrop.

"*Bovis stercus!* That's not how it happened!" Saturn looks disgusted.

"Well, who do you think cares about that now?" Janus gestures into the store, where shoppers line up to buy gift-wrapped Janus Primus watches. "You have not seen it all yet, my friend.

This campaign debuted last month. The company will be rolling out its newest advertisement soon."

"And it is a worse mockery than this?"

"Far worse, my brother. Far worse."

"I still don't understand why we are pairing men with men and women with women. I thought this was a commercial about speed dating for a specific type of clientele?"

Opalia Moneta squirms in her screening room seat. Her creative director, Franco Bellini, and her manager of operations, Marco Bruno, sit opposite her. Various other employees sit or stand along the back wall watching the takes.

"It's a speed dating *concept*," says Franco, trying to keep the frustration out of his voice. "We're trying to show how all the ancient Roman gods had a Greek equivalent, except Janus. He stands alone on the dais, above the rest, and is the unique, omnipotent Roman god. No one can match him. It's the message we're trying to convey about the men who wear our watches."

"Yes, thank you, Franco, I'm not stupid. I get your grand concept." Opalia stands up and gestures at the screen.

Marco turns to Franco. "I agree with Opalia. Why not have Aphrodite fawn over Hercules or have Vulcan offer a glass of wine to Hera?"

Heat colors Franco's face. "Hera is the Greek version of Juno, and Juno is Vulcan's mother, that would never work!"

"*Che cazzo è?!* Who cares?" Opalia stomps her foot, then takes a deep breath to soften her tone. "Look, Franco, we all appreciate this mythology idea you came up with. It's been a hugely successful campaign. We're in the home stretch. Just give me a little variety in addition to what we have already, *mi capisci?*"

Two gentlemen appear in the doorway of the screening room. Opalia can see her secretary behind them, looking aghast.

She doesn't recognize the men and can't imagine how they got into her office suite. One man is tall and exceedingly handsome, with a brilliant smile. The other is short and stocky and clearly older – he is leaning on a cane – but still has a full head of disheveled, long curly hair.

"Greetings, Opalia Moneta. We beg your indulgence for the interruption," says the good-looking man, bending forward slightly at the waist. "This is a matter of utmost importance. In fact, it involves this very advertisement you currently discuss with your team."

"Who the hell are you and how did you get in here?" Opalia is more curious than angry, but her tone is cross nonetheless.

"Allow me to introduce myself and my business associate," the good-looking man says as he enters the room. "My name is Emil Sartori, and this is Jaggo Gianicolo. We are the legal representatives for The Janiculum Trust, a revered institution kept alive generation after generation since the Golden Age of Rome. The main function of the Trust is to protect the interests of the descendants of the Janiculum's founder. Mr. Gianicolo is one of those descendants."

Emil pauses, but Opalia and her team give only confused looks, so he continues.

"Mr. Gianicolo and I are here today to inform you that your advertisements, particularly your use of the image of our founder, Janus, is a violation of the Trust's trademark rights. Opalia Moneta, we are aware that an honorable businesswoman such as yourself would never knowingly break the law, so we bring this to your attention now with the full expectation that you will cease any uses of these images."

As Emil finishes, he again bows slightly. Opalia laughs. "Your founder?! Janus?!" She turns to Marco and Franco. "Is this some kind of joke? Whose idea was this? Did my asshole brothers put you up to this?"

Marco, mouth agape, and palms turned upward, manages to shrug his shoulders. Franco is more direct.

"This is absurd. Who are you people, really?"

"I assure you, Mr. Bellini, we are who we say we are," says Emil. "Ms. Moneta, I've taken the liberty of providing your lawyers with all the requisite documents. Mr. Gianicolo and I will return this evening to finalize arrangements." Flashing a charming smile, and giving one last bow, Emil turns and walks from the room. Jaggo limps out after him.

There is silence in the room until Opalia turns and sits back down at the table. She looks at Marco and Franco, and then at the nameless staff at the back of the room.

"This. Is. Fucking. Brilliant!" Each word is tapped on the table like a drumbeat. Opalia's energy seems electrified. "Whoever came up with this idea is just a fucking genius! Someone call down to security and make sure we get a picture of those two 'lawyers' leaving the building. Marco, make sure we're tweeting about this every hour. And set a press conference for early tomorrow morning. Imagine! Being sued by the so-called descendants of Janus! This will be the best marketing campaign we've ever had!"

Well before the arranged hour, Janus arrives at the Palazzo della Civiltà Italiana in the business district, south of the city center, where he and Saturn will deliver their requests to Opalia. The sun has already set. He stands at the bottom of the podium stairs that form the base of the building. To the right and left are equestrian statues representing the Dioscuri, twin sons of Jupiter, grandsons of Saturn.

"Castor, *bliteus belua es*, you're a beastly idiot," Janus speaks to the sculpture on the left-hand side of the steps. "Are you forever regretting that you let Pollux talk you into becoming immortal?"

Janus looks at the top of the stairs – pictures himself there – and in no time, he is there. He tilts his head sharply to survey the building, uplit by hidden lights in the landscaping. This iconic "Square Colosseum," conceived by Benito Mussolini in the 1930s and completed during the Second World War, stood empty for over a decade after fascism lost its gamble. Since the restoration of the neoclassical landmark, glamour giant Fendi has taken it over as its headquarters, and sublet office space to other Italian luxury brands, most notably a certain family-owned company that Janus plans to enlist in his bid to end his existence. The fact that this company specializes in timepieces is an irony not lost on him.

Janus enters the building and sits on a bench in the open-air loggia. His eyes sweep the cold travertine walls. He allows his hind-sighted face to look east and his fore-sighted face to look west. In both directions, he can see the surrounding logia and the shadowed silhouettes of marble statuary, under arches that are both classical and modern. All twenty-eight of the statues surrounding the building – men and women in time-honored Hellenistic poses – were designed to represent concepts like heroism, music, labor, philosophy, and commerce. From where Janus sits, his view is blocked from all but two: history and military genius. He thinks this an auspicious sign.

Janus contemplates the current scene: himself, a god, at the midway point between two open, arched gates, exactly the same as the image used for the wristwatch advertisement. Resentment rises like bile in his throat. Numa Pompilius designed the open gates of war that adorn the Temple of Janus, eliciting the curse that has kept Janus trapped in the world of men. The same cursed gates will be Janus's ticket out of the purgatory of immortality, however, if he can only convince someone to close them. Not an easy feat, considering the temple's gates disintegrated long ago.

Janus sees Saturn arrive, already in the guise of Emil Sartori. He is thankful for his good-natured and smooth-talking friend. Janus realizes for the first time that when he finally dies, he will miss Saturn dearly.

"*Salve*, Janus! Why have I caught you looking so despondent? Your problem will soon be solved. No more ad campaign!"

"My friend, I surely am not despondent. I was just thinking how grateful I am to you and your honey-tongued abilities. I could not achieve the desired end of this project without you. I am in your debt." Janus rises from the bench, becoming Jaggo Gianicolo.

Opalia waits in a large conference room with Marco, Carlo, and the company's legal team. A few young staffers sit around the perimeter of the room, each clicking on their smartphones. As Emil and Jaggo enter, Opalia makes formal introductions, and they all sit at the oversized mahogany table, upon which are several tall stacks of documents.

"Mr. Sartori, Mr. Gianicolo," says Opalia, smiling broadly. "You took us quite by surprise this morning, but now we've had a little time to acquaint ourselves with your Janiculum Trust. I'm sympathetic to the case you introduced, but my lawyers here are dubious. We require additional time to read through the volumes you provided. In the meantime, perhaps you could tell us more about the Trust, and why you believe our advertising campaign has legal ramifications for you."

Emil beams and rises from his seat, gently pushing away the heavy leather chair behind him. He casts his arms wide, looking as if he is accepting an award instead of defending a position.

"Ms. Opalia Moneta, as I explained earlier, The Janiculum Trust was formed a very long time ago."

The staffers sitting behind the lawyers begin taking pictures of Emil with their phones. He speaks louder and gestures wider and smiles his most charming smile.

"As you can see from the lineage noted in the first addendum," says Emil, gesturing toward the stack of documents, "the descendants of Janus go back to remote antiquity. The second addendum quotes the Aeneid, wherein Virgil describes Janus's founding of pre-Trojan Rome, along with his dear friend Saturn, through the creation of two neighboring towns."

Emil paces the edge of the long table.

"Virgil explains, 'The name of this one was Janiculum, that one, Saturnia.' Hundreds of years later, Macrobius – whose text you can read in addendum three – describes how their descendants called two successive months after them so that December contains the festival of Saturn, and the other, January, contains the name of Janus. It was at this point that the descendants decided they needed to protect the ideals upon which Janus founded the city."

Opalia takes notes, the staffers peck at their phones, and the lawyers simply look on with a mixture of disdain and boredom. Saturn ramps up his rhetoric.

"Take heed of addendum four," Emil proclaims loudly, "for it quotes Plutarch, who describes our founder as a 'patron of civil and social order and is said to have lifted human life out of its bestial and savage state. For this reason, he is represented with two faces, implying that he brought men's lives out of one sort of condition and into another.' The Trust itself formed so that this philosophy would not be adulterated, that men's lives could continue to evolve forwardly, and that the personification of Janus, in the abstract or no, would not be used to thwart his grand notion of humanity."

"So, help me understand," says one of the lawyers. "Are you implying that purchasing and wearing one of our wristwatches – some of which, I must point out, cost as much as an automobile – would cause someone to revert to a 'bestial and savage state?'"

"On the contrary, *amico mio*," replies Emil. "Your company produces timepieces of the utmost quality, I am certain. We, the arbiters of The Janiculum Trust, merely wish to express to you that Janus's image must not be tainted with commerce. He was, is, and will always remain an essential element to the grand design of humanity, in that his dual nature affords the opportunity – nay, the necessity! – for human beings to aspire to see through the gateway he personifies. His conceptual presence holds open a seam in the fabric of the universe, protecting the passageway between the mortal and the celestial, ushering man's worldly view into the possibilities of the divine. That is why he is known as the god of gateways, and why the first month of the year – when mortals aspire to be better than they were in the year past – is named after him."

Janus had heard all this before. He never fully understood Saturn's lofty opinion about the role he plays in the Pantheon and the realm of mortals. Janus is the god of gateways, yes; of beginnings, yes. But Saturn had always imbued Janus's persona with such rarified meaning that it makes him uncomfortable now to hear Saturn's soaring speech. He looks around the room to see how the others receive it.

Although Opalia, Marco, and Franco are smiling, the lawyers do not seem impressed.

"*Actori incumbit onus probation*," says the second lawyer smugly. "In Latin, that means, 'on the plaintiff rests the proving.' You can't honestly believe you could bring a case like this to court?"

"*Salus populi suprema lex esto*," Emil retorts. "Sir, as I'm sure you know, in Latin that means, 'The good of the people shall be the supreme law.' Justice will prevail, I assure you, no matter how long it takes."

"Can we just land this plane?" asks another lawyer. "What exactly is it you want? We've been public with this campaign for over a month."

"If you'll allow me," Jaggo interrupts. Janus has taken the room by surprise because he hasn't spoken a word until now. Even Saturn is a bit startled. "I believe I can suggest a *quid pro quo*, an outcome that would be beneficial to us all."

Almost in unison, cell phones are raised, and pictures snapped. Janus hesitates – he hates being in the limelight – but he presses on.

"For quite some time, my compatriots and I, the other descendants, those of us in the Janiculum Trust…" Janus stammers. He takes a deep breath. "We have a keen interest in restoring the Temple of Janus. The very one your company is depicting in your advertising campaign. I am authorized to put forth the following proposal, which will allow you to continue your campaign while also furthering the interests of the Trust."

Janus can feel Saturn staring at him. He's aware that Saturn may think this move as fickle at best, and a betrayal at worst. Without looking over at his friend, Janus continues.

"If you'll allow me to provide some context regarding the temple, this request will ultimately seem more logical, and I hope more beneficial to you than a commercial about gods who are speed dating."

Opalia exchanges a glance with her art director. Franco crosses his arms over his chest and leans back in his chair.

"By all means, enlighten us," Franco says.

"The temple was built by Numa Pompilius. He was ancient Rome's second king after Romulus founded the city. He tried to instill a sense of peaceful dignity and reverence in his warlike Roman subjects by building temples and promoting religion.

Pompilius stipulated that the temple's gates would be closed in peacetime and remain open in wartime. During his reign, the gates indeed stayed closed, but his successor brought war to the country, and the gates then remained open for hundreds of years."

Janus knows this information is obscure trivia. He needs to bring someone over to his side. "Mr. Franco Bellini, your creative genius is at the heart of this campaign. You seem a scholar of ancient Roman and Greek history, mythology at least. Are you familiar with this story?"

Franco unfolds his arms and leans forward.

"Actually, I did some research on the temple while planning this campaign," Franco says. "Wasn't it after the deaths of Antony and Cleopatra that the gates were closed again, after the Battle of Actium?"

"Indeed," responds Janus as Jaggo. "But they didn't stay closed for long. Throughout history, various emperors opened and closed the gates, both to great fanfare. But war seems to have prevailed as the favored status of civilization, and the gates stayed open almost constantly. Now they no longer exist, so it's as if humanity has no choice but to remain in a constant state of war, with no hope of peace."

"So, Mr. Gianicolo," says Opalia, "if we restore the temple, which would include reproducing the two gates, hanging them in the archways, and closing them, then the Janiculum Trust will have no problem with our ad campaign?"

"It does sound like that is what Mr. Gianicolo is saying," says Emil, glaring at Janus. "But the Trust would continue to 'have a problem' with the campaign if it continues its present course of making gods of vanity and materialism at Janus' expense."

"What about this idea?" says Marco excitedly. "What if we host a huge event – let's say New Year's Eve – that would be perfect! And we put the gates back on, announcing that we're ushering peace back into the world, 'to great fanfare' as you mentioned. Franco, you can have your team design the gates – we've got craftsman in the city that can make them. The media will eat it up!"

Opalia sets down her pen. "Marco, I love this, I do, but New Year's Eve is less than two weeks away. Can we do it in that short a time?"

"This will require a staggering amount of maneuvering," says the smug lawyer. "The Ministry of Public Works, the Archeological Restoration Board, the Cultural Ministry…"

"Do not worry," says Jaggo. "The Janiculum Trust will clear the way. Consider the gates phase one of the restoration project, and by all means, New Year's Eve does sound like the perfect occasion."

No more Januarys for me, thinks Janus. So far, his plan is working perfectly.

Janus and Saturn walk out of the Palazzo della Civiltà Italiana and descend the stairs, past the statues of Saturn's grandsons, by the time Saturn breaks the silence between them.

"What are you playing at, Janus?"

"What do you mean? I just thought the idea with the gates was a way to get the mortals to pay respectful homage to the old ways, and not just dally with them as a curiosity."

"Oh? And what of your 'comfortable anonymity?'"

"It was gone already, my friend. At the service of selling over-priced wristwatches. Why not, as they say, make hay while the sun shines, eh?"

"Hmmm. Well, I have a proposal then," says Saturn. "Let us take the original gate hinges and have them reworked in Vulcan's forge. He can enhance them with his own special powers. Then the temple will indeed be a blend of old and new."

"You know I will not step foot in Vulcan's forge," says Janus, jabbing his cane at the ground. "Have you forgotten the row we had over him heating that underground spring? How he killed those men, those Sabines, who only wanted to rescue their kidnapped daughters? How this 'triumph' was laid at *my* feet?"

"Oh, of course. Yes, I had quite forgotten. Well, I'll handle this for you myself then, my brother."

Janus thanks him. His relief about the success of his plan is so great that it doesn't occur to him that Saturn never forgets anything.

They walk, silent again.

"Do you think all this will happen by New Year's Eve?"

Janus receives no response. It is then he realizes Saturn has disappeared.

It's New Year's Eve, 11:00 p.m. The park-like Roman Forum has not seen a party so elaborate in hundreds of years. It is more of a festival, really, with multiple events spread across its many acres. One stage sits among the ruins of the Basilica Fulvia-Amelia, where a world-renowned tenor is expected to appear at any moment. Hundreds of people are waiting there, and more spill out onto the Via Sacra. On the grassy field in front of the House of the Vestal Virgins, a troupe of acrobats all dressed in white moves lithely among the party-goers. Some are juggling wands like giant sparklers while others walk on their hands tossing glowing spheres to each other with their feet. Images of their performances stream around the world via professional video footage and amateur camera phones. Several photographers turn their attention to a woodwind parade that enters through the Arch of Titus and traverses its course across the Forum to the Arch of Septimus Severus.

Janus watches all of the festivities on the enormous video screens placed throughout the Forum. He marvels at the magnitude of these events that came together in such a short time. His most fervent attention, however, is upon the numerous international journalists and camera operators broadcasting live from positions close to the Curia Julia. This ideal location gives them line-of-sight to the Temple of Janus, where they plan to capture the closing of the gates at midnight. The work crews there, hired to lift the heavy gates into place, are milling around expectantly yet empty-handed. There are no gates yet to position.

Janus feels a twinge of panic. What if the gates don't arrive in time? He's not sure what will happen if they aren't closed by the time December becomes January. Janus edges closer to a knot of people watching a journalist interview Opalia Moneta. He sees that Saturn, in his guise of Emil Sartori, is there, too. Opalia must have been asked about the whereabouts of the much-publicized gates because she is assuring the journalist that they will be arriving any minute.

"The final touches were put on the gates just a short while ago. We were delighted to receive as a gift from the Janiculum Trust," Opalia smiles coquettishly at Emil, "two sets of hinges that were forged by a blacksmith from the Temple's original hardware, excavated from the site over a hundred years ago, along with two exquisite handles that are replicas of the original. The Trust also requested an inscription be carved onto both gates. It's very special. I can't wait for you all to see them."

Janus knew about the hardware but is surprised by the inscriptions. He wonders why Saturn hadn't mentioned this to him.

"Where did you find materials to make gates this large, that could be used for the Janus Temple?" asks the journalist.

"Well," Opalia laughs, "let me tell you, we thought we were stumped! Nothing big enough or strong enough could be found in time for this event. But then I remembered that I had something right in my conference room that could be used! My great, great grandfather had an exquisite table made from a giant tree growing on the Palatine Hill. We decided that the Timepieces for Peace campaign was such a worthy cause, that we cut the table in half and made two gates from it! We banded them with iron and then put the hardware on today. A master craftsman was flown in from Greece to carve the inscription. I'm told the gates are on their way over here right now! This is all very exciting, isn't it?!"

The interviewer doesn't answer and instead turns to Emil. "Mr. Sartori, can you tell us why this Trust, this Janiculum Trust no one has ever heard of before, would want gates put on this old temple?"

"There are those who believe that humanity is a lost cause, that even though they may desire peace, people lack the conviction to hold on to it," he begins, looking directly at Janus in the crowd. "Although this may have been the pattern for hundreds, and even thousands of years, change is inevitable. Recall that this place where we stand was once low-lying swampland, then the center of commerce, and then the birthplace of modern politics. As one age passed and decayed, a new age was built on top of it."

Emil's smile mesmerizes the journalist as he continues. "You've noticed all the restoration activity in Rome, no? And look around! Here are people from all over the world, and more watching through media broadcasts, who are inspired by the idea of peace. So, if putting gates on the Temple of Janus and closing them will symbolize the people's hope for peace, then I'm all in favor of this activity."

A wail of sirens cuts through the reverie. The camera crews rush towards the traffic-jammed Via dei Fori Imperiali to capture footage of a convoy of vehicles arriving. The police escorts have managed to open a path for a large delivery truck, out of which jump several brawny men. With the camera crews' industrial lighting to keep them from fumbling in this dark area outside the Forum, and with Franco Bellini's amplified directions through a megaphone, the men unload first one wooden gate and then the other to much cheering and fanfare. The men in the temple set to work right away.

"We will do the best we can," the foreman tells the journalist who has pushed a microphone into his face to ask about the quickly approaching midnight deadline. "This should have been started hours ago. We're matching new gates and new hardware to ancient posts – if it's off by a fraction of a centimeter, the gates won't hang correctly."

Janus's heart pounds. He looks at the massive Janus Primus clock that has been placed on the temple's pediment: 11:40 p.m. They'll never make it in time, he thinks. His throat feels hot and raw. He tries to slow his breathing.

"What exactly is it that bothers you about this advertising campaign?"

Janus nearly loses his balance as he whirls to see Saturn standing behind him. When he doesn't answer, Saturn continues.

"I believe you are not so concerned about mortals making a mockery of our traditions, as you professed. Janus, you above us all are the most honorable. Do not discredit me now by speaking with a false mouth."

Janus is silent for several moments. Saturn has indeed been a friend to him, and he cannot help but feel a pang of guilt for tricking him into this situation.

Janus moves closer to him. "You know me well, my friend. Although I don't understand how you can laud me with honor for I deserve no such praise. My lack of courage in sharing the truth merely points to the loss of it in all aspects of my life." He stares at the second hand on the giant clock. "You asked what bothers me most about this circus of a wristwatch campaign. The truth is, nothing bothers me about it. Not one thing. I do not care about it, as I do not care about anything anymore. It was just a means to an end."

"*Ohē!* Janus, I believe you believe this, but I do not. *Temet nosce!* Know thyself! I will ask you again: What bothers you the most?"

Janus tries to regain his footing. He clears his mind and probes his deepest self. What bothers him? An image comes to him immediately. He sees the shop window panorama of the Sabine women, cheering along with their captors after their fathers and brothers and husbands were murdered for simply trying to rescue them. He remembers clearly how it really happened, so long ago. He was not trying to keep the men out by barring the gate; he was trying to open it to let them in. History twisted this sick moment into something heroic, and an entire city was founded upon it. Try as he might, he cannot stop the tears from rolling down his face. He feels foolish for this emotion, realizing he is still carrying it after so very many years.

"It is the Sabines, is it not?" asks Saturn.

"How could you know?"

"I have always known. To be honest, I have felt guilt for being part of that story, that campaign to found Rome. I know you had a love for those people as you have for all mortals. But it was necessary. Or, it seemed so at the time." Saturn gently takes Janus's face into his hands. "It was wrong. Can you forgive me?"

Janus looks at Saturn and shakes his head free, backing away from him. "Of course, I forgive you. It never occurred to me that you were at fault in any way."

"Thank you, Janus. This is why I say you have the most integrity of all the gods. You are truly good. You are loving and trusting."

Janus searches for a thread in the argument to avoid softening his resolve. "Perhaps once I loved mortals. *O quantum est in rebus inane*, so much futility. Nothing ever changes. They are just hopeless."

Saturn nods, clasping his hands in front of him. "Perhaps humans have disappointed you, Janus. You close the gates of your heart to not feel it, convince yourself you do not care. But what is worse? To feel disappointment or doom? Humanity is in a constant state of creation, and if you keep yourself open to them, they will surprise you."

Janus wants to believe what Saturn is saying but does not feel connected to it. "Perhaps, my friend," says Janus. "Perhaps it is true. I hope that you are right. But I still feel my time here has passed. I am old, I am not needed, and I do not belong. I need these temple gates to be closed" – he faces the clock: 11:55 – "so the curse will be lifted, and I can finally close my eyes to all of this."

Saturn sighs deeply. "Janus, I don't suppose it would occur to you that, having divined your plan, I might sabotage the gate hinges? Knowing what's best for you, I would incur your wrath so that you might reinvest in the world of the living?"

Janus spins toward Saturn. He is astounded at his naïveté. How could he not have considered this as a possibility?

"Listen to me," Saturn reassures him. "There was no need. The only curse that ever existed was the one you placed on yourself. It has made you look too much to the past and not enough to the future. And you spend no time in the present."

Janus is speechless, trying to process Saturn's words.

Saturn turns to go. "My friend, you can kill a man. Maybe you can even kill a god. But you cannot kill an idea if it is kindled in even one person." Saturn looks back at his friend. "Janus, you must accept the fact that you are an Idea. The embodiment of hope. You are here to stay."

The good news ripples through the crowd – the gates fit! – and then spreads around the world to all those watching. At 11:59, the last worker steps away, hammer in hand, to let Franco Bellini take his place. Marco Bruno stands at the other gate, while Opalia Moneta rushes to stand in the center of the Temple. She looks for Emil Sartori but gives up as the countdown begins.

The crowd surges toward the Temple to catch a glimpse of the gates closing. In unison, they shout along with Opalia, "Ten…nine…eight…"

Franco and Marco grab ahold of their gate handles and pull. Marco's gate moves easily, but Franco's will not budge.

"Seven…six…"

The workmen scurry to Franco's gate and shove the massive door, imploring it to move.

"Five…four…"

A loud groan sounds as the hinge surrenders to the workmen's force. The gate swings to a close.

"Three…two…one!"

The world-famous tenor sings on cue, but fireworks drown his voice. People in the crowd weave among one other, shaking hands, hugging, and sharing *il Bacio*, the famous Italian cheek kiss.

The hinges hold. The gates close and do not collapse.

It is now January 1, and if Janus is still alive, it must mean that Saturn was correct: there never was a curse. Could this feeling he feels possibly be relief? This is quite surprising, he thinks.

Perhaps then, his old friend is also correct about humanity. If they are in a constant state of creation, why not wait and see what good may come of it?

Janus approaches the newly closed gates to see the inscription Saturn chose. It is a message to him from his oldest friend, one that resonates whether the gates are open or closed:

Ex agape spes. Ex spe pax.

From love, hope. From hope, peace.

February

LA PETITE MORT

Benjamin Carr

There was cruelty in the air. Georgia humidity was no joke. It intended those in the amphitheater to suffer. The contestants onstage in their formalwear probably had it the worst, for they also had the pink-glazed stage lights to contend with and the pressures of gentility. The whole thing was a debacle for us judges and the hand-fanning folks in the audience, too. However, no one questioned why this "professional" beauty pageant was happening outdoors at 4:30 p.m. on a Tuesday in July. The truth about the pay-to-play event, the free venue, and its corrupt organizers would come later, after my mishap. While the contest was going on, we all had to put our best faces on and pretend we were happy to be there. Never mind the heat. Never mind the sweat. That's show business.

I was wearing more makeup than anyone else and my own version of an oppressive costume, but no one ever thinks about my comfort. The organizers of Miss Georgia Sweetheart 1982 didn't even know my fucking name. In the mimeographed programs, I was listed as *Judge #2: Morty the Midget Clown!*

Professionally, I'm just Morty the Clown, damn it.

That misprint is what the newspaper called me in its next edition, too, when they ran my picture next to Contestant 6's. The photos made us both look unassuming, despite what the headline stated about the crime.

Pictures lie.

• • • •

I'm jumping the gun in the way that I'm telling you this. Let me back up.

You're getting it exclusive from me, by the way. I'm not going to tell anybody else the truth about that day. Not the papers. Not the cops. Nobody.

Most clowns don't do much talking, anyway. It lessens the effect. They tell us to keep mute at Ringling Brothers. Fuck Ronald McDonald and Bozo and all that noise. Clarabell had it right. Stay mute. It's one of the few things respectable about mimes.

If you heard my voice, sounding all West Texas gruff, middle-aged and pissed off, you wouldn't let your kids near me. Even at 4-foot-8.

But if you open a pageant with me all tiny and cuddly, circling the stage with a painted-on smile while riding a tricycle like a perpetual toddler, the children laugh, and the parents cheer. My innocent white face. My eyebrows. My giant green bow tie. My squeaky horn. My cue ball head. All the folks that are there to root for their sister or cousin love that I'm acting foolish. They love that I'm handing out Brown Cow bars from an oversized purse. I'm good at my job. I can even do it half-drunk onstage at this fucking amphitheater.

God damn it, why didn't I just fucking sleep in or go to the Tattletale with the rest of the troupe? I was the only clown dumb enough to accept a $50 appearance fee on our one night off from this week's shows at the Omni. It would've spared everyone the grief.

The organizers just wanted someone from the circus to be there. They wanted trapeze artists or female acrobats, the kind of performer these girls could aspire to be - if they worked on their flexibility and kink. But they settled for me – a different kind of entertainment. Because I'm a joke.

According to the program, the other judges were also pulling double duty as both pageant critic and performer. Rev. Green's wife opened with "an invocation" - five Bible verses and a prayer – underneath a misspelled banner: "MISS GOERGIA SWEETHEART 1982." The Z93 radio DJ served as both emcee and judge. And the fucking fag chorus teacher sang Manilow between the contestant introductions and the swimsuit competition. The crowd ate it up.

Technically, my tricycle bit didn't even qualify as part of the show. The emcee called me on stage only to pacify the audience while the girls from Lilburn and Lawrenceville waxed off their mustaches.

A gig is a gig is a gig.

The swimsuit competition was when I first really noticed the girl. She wore a blue sash with the number 6 on it, over a pink polka-dotted one-piece that made me wonder if her nipples matched the suit.

Onstage, I circled all the contestants a couple of times on my tricycle, misting them with a spray bottle. It was an improvised idea. The emcee was just trying to stop folks from leaving and stop the girls from having a heat stroke. I had my choice of contestants, but the girl with sash #6 had some fight in her. I could see it. The whole affair annoyed her. She rolled her eyes at the emcee. She read that misspelled banner and winced.

So, I blasted Contestant 6 in both the front and the back, making her twitch from the unexpected spray of cold water. Feisty girls respond when you tease them. I liked her wet and quivering. She glared at me in frustration, but she kept her plastered-on smile.

My eyes were keen. Contestant 6 was a natural redhead. God may have cursed me with this tiny body, but at least I can appreciate the view.

That should've been the end of it. A few brazen moments of pleasant teasing, her sexualization on full display in front of a crowd that viewed me as a deformed, retarded child. Some girl would've been crowned the winner. I would've collected my fifty bucks and gone back to the Greatest Show on Earth. I never would've spoken to Contestant 6.

But one of the other contestants walked out wearing a white bikini, and Rev. Green started having trouble breathing. (That contestant was a member of his congregation or some shit. I don't know exactly. Some part of him probably wanted to fuck her. And it wasn't the part that he usually let the public see.) The crowd started to rustle. Mrs. Green started praying, either for her husband's life or death. I'm not sure. Somebody went to get a medic. I was directed to pedal my ass backstage, leading the girls off for a forced intermission from 5:30 to who-the-fuck-knows. Once we were backstage, most of the girls headed to the dressing room to gossip.

Not her, though. She caught sight of who must have been her mother, hairbrush in hand and a frown on her face, gesturing for Contestant 6 to take a seat. I saw her too. The woman was dressed like a real estate agent on portrait day. Contestant 6 flipped off her mother, a gesture that caused the prim lady to scamper, then headed to the cigarette machine meant for farmhands and stagehands – not pretty girls in a pageant.

Then, she propped open the back door with a brick.

We both smoke Winstons. That's how I ended up entangled with the polka-dotted cunt.

●   ●   ●   ●

She was a breath of fire on an already hot day, reclined on a towel across the top of an unpainted wooden picnic table just outside the backdoor entrance. Her hair fanned out across the table top. She'd stashed her sash somewhere, probably in the dressing room. She held the lit cigarette between her fingers on her right hand, which hung over the table's edge. She occasionally lifted the cigarette to her lips to take a drag, some elaborate gesture she learned from old movies, but she otherwise kept it away from her body. A dropped cherry might leave a mark.

Contestant 6's left arm covered her eyes, shielding them from the sun. She didn't see me approach.

I made my way to the table and took a seat on the bench; her body spread in front of me like a chicken dinner.

I coughed, and she removed her arm to look at me. There was a dusting of peach fuzz along her forearm. Most girls probably would've screamed, afraid of clowns. Contestant 6 just smirked.

"Where's your trike?" she asked.

"Parked backstage," I replied. "Why aren't you?"

"Because that's where the other girls are," she admitted.

"You don't like them?"

"If you were a girl, you wouldn't either."

I chuckled.

"You don't sound like you look," she said.

"We don't all speak in falsetto," I told her. "But my nose squeaks if you touch it."

Her pack of cigarettes lay on the table near her waist. She caught me looking at it, so she rolled on her side and offered me one. The cigarette moved from my miniature hand to my painted smile. Then I pulled a chain of nine multicolored, tied-together handkerchiefs and a Zippo out of my pocket.

At that, Contestant 6 laughed so hard she had to sit up. I wiggled my eyebrows. The old jokes are the most effective.

When she laughed, that's when she seemed more like a girl to me. I liked her better that way.

She liked me, too. She sat at the edge of the table and put her feet beside me on the bench.

"I never knew redheads could tan," I said. "I thought they just went from pale to burnt."

She regarded me warily, just like every other natural redhead.

"I never knew they made tricycles for grown-ups," she said. "I guess we're all learning something new today."

I tensed. Her statement stung more than it should have, perhaps because she could see my age.

"Actually, I'm covered in ridiculous amounts of sunblock right now," she said. "I'm surprised you can't see how white it looks on my legs."

I accepted the invitation to take in her gams up close. I'd already done so without permission, but she opened the door for more. She knew what she was doing.

"Eh, it's not as white as what I have on," I said.

She leaned in for a better look, her locks falling to the side of her face. Her eyes were blue. Our cigarettes rested on the table, slowly burning down to the filters. We were on to better things.

My entire bald head was painted white as a Klansman's robe. My eyebrows, three lines, penciled all the way up to my forehead. My lips were painted in a large, red, silly oval.

"I hadn't noticed that the makeup was so detailed," she said. "Is that a beauty mark?"

She pointed at my cheek.

"Yup," I said.

She moved closer to me, our faces almost touching. She turned her head to puzzle at my cheek. Her breath smelled like Winston-Salem.

"It's a heart," she said. *"No way ... "*

I smiled at her.

"It's a Sweet Heart," I told her. "I take the candy. I put it on my clown white. It leaves an impression. Then, I just paint in the color."

"Do people notice that kind of small touch?" she asked, hovering so close I could feel her body heat.

And then I pinched her leg.

Her blue eyes flared – startled and violated. She opened her mouth to say something, but her words remained unspoken. I kept my fingers where they were, squeezing her slippery thigh a little harder. I bet she liked it. It must have been such a foreign experience for her.

I let her go after a beat or two.

"Thank you," she whispered to me.

"For touching you?" I asked. "Or for stopping?"

Contestant 6 considered this but said nothing. She looked at the door, nervous.

"You're curious, aren't you?" I teased her.

She changed the topic.

"I'm surprised no one's come to find us," she said. "The reverend must be really bad off."

"I know he is," I said. "I met his wife."

Contestant 6 didn't laugh. She didn't get it.

Most people don't know what to do with their urges. They suppress them. They deny their natural inclinations. It's unhealthy, I think. Of course, I'm different from most people. I'm less inclined to give a fuck. People expect strangeness when they look at me.

If I waited for someone else to make a move, I'd still be a virgin.

"You don't know much about men, do you?" I asked.

She eyed me as if I were a nuisance.

"Most of the boys your age don't pay you any mind, do they?" I continued. "They see you, and they don't know what to think. A beautiful thing like you left unattended."

"I don't like people my age," she said defiantly.

"So, you try to be older than, what, 16?" I concluded. "You smoke your dad's cigarettes. You only do shit shows like this one if your mom makes you, but you don't care about winning. You don't even want to be here. You don't know what you want – only what you don't. I knew a girl like you once on the road. A real rebel. You're the kind that breaks rules – and hearts."

She glanced at the ground.

"I even talk to strangers," she said.

"I noticed that."

Kids don't know when to walk away from trouble. They want to be liked. She raised her eyes to meet mine, ready to prove me wrong.

I wasn't wrong.

Her tone perked up.

"Mister, what about you?" she asked. "How old are you?"

"44."

"Nothing better to do than talk to me?"

"Nope."

"44. That's my mom's age," she scoffed.

"And what is she doing with her day?"

"Probably wondering where I am, *sir*."

"Go find her then," I said. "I'll see you when the show starts back."

Contestant 6 didn't move.

"Go on," I urged.

Still nothing.

Then she grabbed my arm, hard.

"I oughta make you pay," she said. "You kept shooting at me with that water bottle like I was a target. Nobody else got hit like I did."

It hurt so good.

"You clearly needed cooling off," I said.

She shoved me.

I smiled at her.

"Stop it," she said.

I started to laugh. She was so cute.

"*Stop it,*" she repeated.

Then she stood up and acted like she was going inside. But the tease knew we weren't done.

I grabbed her ass.

She looked alarmed.

"You don't want me to stop anything," I said. "I'm a curiosity, and you're curious."

I smacked her on the polka dots.

She froze right there and let me give it to her. I spanked her. One slap; two slaps. If she didn't want it, she could've left.

"You're gonna leave a mark," she said, annoyed. "The other judges will see. Stop doing that."

"I can do something else," I muttered.

My hand slipped from her backside, traveling elsewhere. She felt me groping the front side of her polka dots, searching for the edge of her swimsuit. She hesitated, then stepped away from me, and bowed her head. I could feel my palm tingle.

She wanted it. I don't care if she says differently. I swear I heard her purr.

"Why did you do that?" she asked, a tremble in her voice.

"I thought you wanted to play with the grown-ups," I told her.

Contestant 6 moved closer, looking down at me.

"I am grown," she said defiantly. It was so precious. She held her head high and grinned.

And, for a moment, our interaction was over. She stepped away and rushed toward the door, back to the safety of the chaperones.

The girl had left her pack on the picnic table, so I helped myself to another cigarette. We still had a pageant to finish, and I wasn't even sure if I was going to vote for her. Whatever had happened between us had certainly been fun for me. But someone who wanted to win would've gone further, you know? Done something to really mess up the lipstick.

But Contestant 6 wasn't interested in winning any pageant, and she was about to prove me right again.

"Hey, Morty!"

I started to turn around, expecting to find that she had gotten her dad. It wouldn't be the first time. Dads don't fight me, though, when they realize I'm smaller than Danny DeVito. My size makes people underestimate me, think that nothing bad can come from such a small package.

I use misconceptions to my advantage. Nobody fears me. Nobody tries to break me. Nobody makes me pay for the "misunderstandings" that happen. Everybody laughs it off and walks away, dragging the girls away with them.

And, for the record, my package ain't that small.

As I turned to look at her, something cracked against the back of my head. I only saw blood and stars. My ears rang in a high pitch.

By the time she came into full view, Contestant 6 had struck me again, the brick in her fist connecting with the heart on my cheek.

My entire jaw crumpled against the force of it. I couldn't help wailing, even though I like it rough. I slumped against the table, my legs still on the bench.

She moaned over my cries.

And she kept at it. The brick against my forehead, then against my chest. Occasionally, she would just claw at me with her left hand.

I was past the ability to resist her. Her strength was impressive.

Her hands were all white by the time she stopped. The brick was pink at the edges, my blood mixing with my clown white. My body slipped from the bench and fell under the table. My head misshapen as a raisin. Contestant 6's body trembled; her mouth curled into a snarl, baring her teeth.

For a moment, she just stood there, her blood-splattered breasts heaving from the effort. Then, she dropped the brick.

No one came outside. No one saw what happened. No one heard me dying. The back door had closed because of the very way the little bitch chose to kill me.

Contestant 6 tucked the bench in under the table, covering my body. The bench rested on top of my sleeve. She turned and went back inside. She had to wash up that torso and change back into a gown before the show started again.

I guess none of the contestants paid her any mind. They didn't see her as a threat.

About ten minutes later, they paged for me over the loudspeaker.

"Morty the Midget, please return to the judges' table," the emcee said. "Morty the Midget, please return to the judges' table!"

They didn't wait long before passing judgment without me.

●   ●   ●   ●

A stagehand discovered my body after the pageant. He carried my tricycle out the back door, then lit a joint for himself. When he pulled out the bench, it dragged my little corpse with it.

The cops brought Contestant 6 in for questioning later that night, picking her up at her parents' house. The pack of Winstons and the brick had her fingerprints all over it. She only denied it for an hour; then she blamed the whole thing on me.

She cried sexual assault. And they bought it. Of course, they did.

I wasn't around to dispute her. Even if I had been, I don't count as a whole person to anybody anyway, so what good would my word have done?

Contestant 6 got almost no time in juvie for my murder.

Nobody wanted to punish the winner of Miss Georgia Sweetheart 1982. She was a nice girl with a bright, promising future.

YOURS, S

Samantha Thomson LoCoco

M ildred steered her station wagon along the narrow serpentine drive, searching for her husband's headstone. One of the directives in Willis's last will and testament requested that a white flag be affixed to the top of his marker. A sign of surrender, he'd called it, something he'd chuckled at, but it chipped away at Mildred's heart each time she looked for it. She'd rather think of her husband as someone who'd fought to stay with her for as long as possible than someone who'd willingly succumbed to such a permanent separation.

Mildred squinted. "Does make you easy to find, though, doesn't it?"

She pulled over onto the gravel turnoff beneath two oak trees, their knotty roots twisting over themselves like wooden waves trapped in the mud. She recalled stumbling over one when Willis brought her to see the plots he'd purchased for them. Such a morbid thing to do, Mildred had thought at the time, but Willis saw it as practical, romantic even. He had a way of loving her she never quite fully understood. *I wouldn't want you to have to think about these things after the fact*, Willis had said. *Too emotional a time to pick out a burial plot, don't you think, Mills? This way, no decisions have to be made – it's all taken care of.* Mildred had thought two things that day: one, why was he so certain he would die first, and, two, what if she *wanted* to make some decisions? She hadn't said anything at the time, but, on the day of Willis's funeral, as she sat in a chair to receive those who'd come to mourn Willis with her, all she could do was curse him. He'd planned for everything, so there was absolutely nothing she could do but hurt, and she had been furious with him for that.

Stepping over the knotted roots, Mildred walked down the grassy aisle toward Willis. The lawn had not been mown due to days of rain, and the blades of grass all but buried her feet as she moved forward, droplets of water slipping off their pointed ends and speckling her stockings. By the time she reached Willis, the droplets had connected across the bridge of her foot in complete dampness. Mildred sighed as she stood facing Willis's tombstone.

"You're looking well," she said. She cocked her head and thought some bundle of rich hewn petals would brighten up the cold marble, but Willis would have none of it. *Don't bring me flowers when I'm dead. All they'll do is wilt and die and who needs the reminder?* Mildred scanned the other plots and noticed only a few bouquets of soggy flowers and felt mildly less guilty for always arriving empty-handed. She tightened the straps of her rain bonnet and clasped her hands in front of her, re-reading the chiseled lettering Willis had chosen: "Here lies Willis Sycamore Oliphant, pretty good husband, and a damn good golfer. March 5, 1928 – July 5, 2008."

Mildred leaned forward and placed her hands at the edges of the stone, just as she had always done with Willis's broad shoulders when she'd wanted him to focus on what she was saying. "Happy birthday, darling," she said, straightening up. Another stipulation of Willis's final request was that she visit him on his birthday and not the anniversary of his death. *I can't imagine it'll be a day you'll want to relive every year.* But to Mildred, the day of her husband's death was her memory alone. He'd only been home from the hospital a day and had been in such good spirits. His eyes had seemed so clear that Mildred was certain he was on the mend. They'd fallen asleep in each other's arms as they did when they were newly married. She'd kissed his forehead in the morning and slipped out of bed to make their tea. By the time she returned, he was still. No teacup shattered. No sharp intake of breath. She simply uttered, "Oh, Willis," and sat beside him on their bed until she was ready to call someone.

In contrast, Mildred had no memory of Willis's birth, though his retelling of it always made her smile. Each year, the legend grew. It started with what his mother's sister had relayed to him each year: a thunderstorm in rural Tennessee caused a widespread blackout and a tree limb to fall, blocking the front door, just as his mother's water broke. She'd waddled out the back door, hoping to find a neighbor at home but on the short walk from her back porch to the backyard, she realized her son was about to make his appearance. Searching for a dry spot, she crawled beneath the canopy of an old sycamore tree and in three swift pushes in rhythm with the rolling thunder, Willis was born.

Over the years, the intensity of the storm grew, the length of labor extended into the wee hours of the morning, and the whereabouts of Willis's father shifted from being deployed to being held up at work to not being a part of the story at all. What remained the same in each version of the story was the resolution: the experience gave Willis his middle name.

When they were dating or "courting" as Willis liked to refer to it, Mildred had taken to calling him Sycamore. At first, it was to tease him. She noticed when he revealed his middle name to her and the story that went with it, he saw that she was skeptical. He'd anticipated a captive audience and instead found a rational woman who'd poked holes in his story. To this day, Mildred believed it's what kept his attention all these years. She saw that he liked the challenge, so calling him Sycamore became a way to entice him – to fold the laundry, to clean the gutters, to come to bed. It was a way for Mildred, who never fully felt comfortable with all that love talk, to, in fact, say "I love you" without having to say it at all.

Willis caught on. He'd leave her notes all over the house. She'd come to the teapot in the morning, and there would be a note taped to it: *My wife's hotter than any teapot. But don't tell her I said so. Yours, S.* When Mildred would reach for her keys, a note sat just above their hook: *Don't forget me. Yours, S.* Pulling wrapped steaks from the freezer to thaw, she'd find written on the packaging: *Moooooooooooo. Yours, S.* Her favorite place to find his notes was tacked to the sycamore tree out back. *Gone fishin'. For fish, not ladies. Yours, S.*

After Willis died, Mildred had resisted the urge to visit the cemetery every single day. She just wanted to be near his body. To talk to him, or perhaps feel his presence. Something the preacher had said at the graveside service stayed with her: "Willis is not here. His body rests while his soul returns home and his memories stay alive in all of us." *Willis is not there*, she would tell herself any time she lifted her keys from their ring to make the long drive westward. For many weeks, she would return the keys to their place and crawl into bed on her husband's side, wondering if maybe this was the home he'd returned to.

One day, instead of walking down the long, dark hallway to their bedroom, Mildred decided to go outside. She thought she might sit on the back porch a while, but she found herself moving into their backyard and leaning against their sycamore tree. At first, she spoke only inside her head, but soon, she had conversations out loud – with the tree, with Willis. Some days she would recount all she had done that day – everything from having the car's oil changed to talking with Aunt Dorothy, she's doing well, by the way – and other days all she could muster was "I miss you." The tree supported her either way.

●   ●   ●   ●

The second year after Willis died was tougher for Mildred because she could no longer think, *this time, last year*. *This time, last year, we were picking apples to make cider for the Fall Festival*. Or, *this time, last year, was the first hospital visit*. Or, *this time, last year, he talked me into staying in bed on a Sunday morning*. He was further away from her now. The only thought that comforted Mildred was that she was old, and they had spent so many decades together, she would always have more days spent with Willis than without him.

She'd visited him again on his birthday this year like he'd asked, and she'd still wanted to bring him flowers, but she didn't. She did spend some time tidying up his plot, wiping off the headstone with her handkerchief and shooing away stray twigs. Mildred looked at the white flag atop Willis's gravestone. It had frayed slightly at its edges but still flapped against the wind like it was supposed to. Mildred smiled and consented that perhaps the flag was a little funny. Dusting off her knees, Mildred surveyed the surrounding plots and, once again, felt some relief that there weren't too many flowers present. A slight pang of guilt passed through her because she thought maybe there weren't many flowers because people don't visit graves anymore. She hoped it was more of a practical reason like Willis's request. People visited but didn't waste money on flowers. That must be it, she thought. She also thought it was strange that all the flowers she did see were red.

"Must be a sale at the Stock nursery," said Mildred. She placed her hands on her husband's tombstone and shared a birthday wish with him before collecting her handbag and walking back to the car.

As she drove up the winding path toward the exit, she saw a few cemetery attendants gathered at the top corner of the field overlooking where Willis lay. They seemed to be watching her car ascend the path until the one with the rake returned to raking and encouraged his cohorts to do the same. As she drove past them, Mildred raised her hand to wave, but none of them looked at her.

"Young people," she muttered as she eased her old station wagon onto the two-lane road that led her home.

On the morning of March 5th, three years after Willis died, Mildred decided to stay home rather than visit her husband's grave. She would go in July, on the anniversary of his death. On the anniversary of the day she remembered with gratitude because her beloved husband had held her all the night through and waited until she had risen for their morning tea before departing. The day when she had held her dead husband's hand and spoken softly to him for a very long time until she felt he had truly left the room.

A morning chill crept into the air. Mildred wrapped herself in one of Willis's old cardigans and took her tea to their back porch. Sitting on the top step, she sipped from her mother's chipped teacup and breathed in the dampness of the morning. She loved days like this. They had always made Willis a bit melancholy; he much preferred the bright sunshine of the later spring and summer months. But, for Mildred, she appreciated when outside matched her insides. She had never considered herself a sad or particularly depressive personality, but solemn might best describe her inner workings. She moved slowly, with a preference to observe the world rather than participate in it, and though one might think that would clash with Willis's sunny demeanor and quick wit, it instead complimented it. She never took the sunshine away from Willis, and he never forced her into it, knowing she preferred a cool, gray day and a hot cup of tea.

Mildred rested her chin in her hand and caught Willis's scent trapped in the fabric of his old sweater: hickory and chamomile. She smiled and buried her nose in the crook of her arm and inhaled. Mildred had always assumed it was his aftershave but learned early on in their marriage that he didn't use any. He used whatever products she brought home for herself but no matter the lavender soap or cocoa butter, he always smelled of hickory and chamomile to her. Like a stamped-out campfire in the wee hours of morning.

Staring at the cement path below her, Mildred followed a crack from the tip of her toe, up the length of the walkway. It climbed the three stone steps near the driveway and widened near the base of the garage to reveal jagged edges of pebbled concrete and undulating ancient roots from the sycamore tree in the center of their backyard. She sighed. She knew she would have to address the issue sooner rather than later, but anyone she'd previously sought help from only suggested to uproot the tree before further damage to her foundation occurred. She'd rather tear down the house than uproot that tree. Still, she questioned her balance daily, so rather than traverse the rocky terrain of the driveway, she'd taken to parking on the street in front of the house.

Willis would be mortified if he knew, thought Mildred. He would never have allowed their car to sit on the street as if they were visiting. *This is our home*, she could hear him say, *and we won't be uprooted by a tree.* She thought he would have more empathy considering it was a sycamore tree. *Wasn't the one I was born under, so it's got no claim over me.* Mildred loved the tree, however. It sat perfectly at the center of their yard as if the whole property had been designed around it. Its dense foliage created canopies of respite in the summer months, and its mottled bark offered a bit of shocking beauty in the barren winters, its upper branches as white as bleached bones. Willis complained ad nauseum about how much the tree shed – irregular pieces of bark, leaves as big as their heads, and spindly seed clusters that stuck to the rake. But it never dampened Mildred's enjoyment of the tree, watching its leaves curl into themselves like dangling handkerchiefs before dropping to the ground, another season ended and begun. The tree had been there for almost a century and, Mildred thought, would most likely outlive them all.

Mildred sipped her tea, her hand unsteady. Her eyes flicked up to one of the sycamore's midline branches to find a bright red cardinal surveying her yard. The bird swooped down and landed on the top stone step at the end of the walkway, then cocked his head and flexed his crest. His fire red feathers starkly contrasted the dark grays and mossy greens of the stones beneath him. The bird hopped down one step, then the next, and took a few confident hops in Mildred's direction. She lowered her teacup and set it beside her.

"Hello."

The cardinal twitched his tail and angled his head so that one black eye looked up at her. His bright orange beak and black mask looked expertly painted, and Mildred thought him to be quite stunning. He pecked at the ground a couple of times, took one more hop toward her, then flew away. She watched him gain height against the backdrop of gray sky and thought that small moments like this one made her grateful to be alive.

By the time the fifth anniversary of Willis's death neared, Mildred had made a compromise with the sycamore tree. She had paid to have her driveway repaved so that it curved around the tree's roots and asked for a new walkway to be designed from the garage to the side entrance of the house so that she wouldn't have to worry about tripping on her way to and from the car. Every morning, she reminded the tree not to mess with the foundation of her home or she would be forced to cut back its roots, and neither of them wanted that.

The cardinal was a regular visitor by now, and he had brought company. Mildred hired the neighbor girls to help rake the yard and hang bird feeders. There were three sisters in all, and Mildred noted that each had their strong suit. The eldest not only hung the bird feeders but designed and built some new ones as well that welcomed birds and deterred squirrels. The middle girl seemed physically stronger than her sisters and enjoyed using her strength to rake the leaves and dispose of the troublesome seed clusters that frequently carpeted Mildred's backyard. She was very organized, too, the middle sister, and Mildred enjoyed watching her process – piling dead leaves near the trash can so she didn't have to carry them far and gathering seed clusters on top of newspapers she'd spread out, making it easier to throw them away. She reminded Mildred a great deal of herself. The youngest sister was still quite small, though her vocabulary was not. She was an excellent conversationalist and enjoyed searching for pieces of bark that matched each of their skin tones, often noting with pride that Mildred's was the darkest among the four of them. On this day, the young girl sat on the step next to Mildred, sipping iced tea, and discussed how she saw the world. The girl didn't need much prompting, and Mildred was happy to listen.

"Now, I don't know how Miss Jean plans to run her classroom next year, but if she won't put a stop to the rampant snack stealing, then I guess I'll have to get to the bottom of it."

The youngest's name was Mae, the same as Mildred's mother, and Mildred smiled about how much her mother would have liked this child. She and Willis tried for children, but none ever came. In the end, she'd been grateful that it had just been the two of them because they got to have each other all to themselves. Mildred had watched her friends and cousins raise loads of children, and she'd been diligent about sending birthday cards and graduation gifts. It was only now, listening to young Mae, that Mildred wondered if her mother had ever been disappointed that she never had grandchildren to listen to.

Mildred told the girls it was time for them to get to their schoolwork so she could go and visit Willis. They all found a stopping point in their endeavors and wished Mildred a good evening. She thanked them for their company and their efforts and pulled three folded up five-dollar bills from her coin purse and handed one to each sister.

"For your ingenuity," Mildred said to the first sister. "For your strength," she said to the second. And, to Mae, she said, "For your thoughts."

Mae wrinkled her nose and wondered aloud whether or not one could buy a person's thoughts to which her eldest sister responded, "What do you think books are?" Mae seemed satisfied by the answer and trotted back to her house. The middle sister followed, wiping her forehead with the back of her wrist.

The oldest sister lingered. "Please say hi to Mr. Oliphant for me."

Mildred looked up at the girl's smooth face and tried to remember her name. "Do you remember him, sweetheart?"

"Yes, ma'am," the girl said, looking at her feet. "He helped me with my math homework."

Mildred smiled, surprised. "Did he?"

The girl nodded. "One night, he came out here and found me behind your tree. I'd run away from home because I had failed another math test." The girl glanced at Mildred, perhaps searching to see if she already knew the story. "Didn't get very far, I guess."

"He was an engineer, my husband," Mildred said. "Forty-five years."

"Yes, ma'am." The girl shifted her feet. "He told me that I couldn't run away from home, that my parents didn't deserve that kind of fright, and that he'd be happy to help me study if it was all right with my folks."

Mildred chuckled. "Did he help you at all?"

"I'm very grateful, ma'am." She nodded once and turned toward her house. Mildred watched her walk away and marveled that she might still learn something new about her husband. She'd always thought he would have made a lovely teacher, and had told him so on many occasions. *Who wants to be around kids all day*, he'd said, *I got my hands full with you.*

Just before Mildred stepped inside to retrieve her keys and her purse, she heard the girl call her name. When Mildred looked up, the girl was standing near her backyard, one foot propping open the gate.

"Math is my favorite subject now, ma'am."

Mildred saw the girl smile before she disappeared into her backyard, and remembered her name was Carol.

On Willis's ninetieth birthday, nearly ten years after his death, Mildred drove silently down the two-lane highway that led to the cemetery. She'd bought some flowers from the corner market before she left; she couldn't help herself. She placed a protective hand over them in the passenger seat as she slowed to let another car pass. Sunlight glared against her window, causing her to squint at the road in front of her.

Mildred was visiting earlier than usual because she planned to attend a luncheon with her bridge club that day, and she couldn't visit after the luncheon because she had to get home in time to start the roast for dinner that evening with Carol. Mildred couldn't believe the girl was graduating this year and felt a flash of sadness that their Monday night dinners were numbered. Carol had been accepted to the civil engineering program at Lipscomb in Nashville, and Mildred couldn't be prouder of her. For her application essay, Carol had written about Willis's tutoring and the friendship she had developed with Mildred after his death. Carol had given a copy to her at one of their recent dinners, and Mildred had brought it with her today to read to Willis.

One Monday evening, not too far back, Mildred had asked Carol to bring her an old cookbook from the top shelf of the pantry. There was a recipe for apple turnover she wanted to send home with Carol for her mother. As they sat at the kitchen table and flipped through the pages, a scrap of loose paper fell out and landed on the floor. Carol reached for it and read aloud as she lifted the paper to the table. *If ever there was a recipe for a perfect match, you and I are it. Yours, S.* Mildred took the note from Carol and traced her fingers over Willis's handwriting. She was taken aback by how tightly the moment had grabbed her. In the first couple of years after his passing, she would find notes hidden all about the house on a fairly regular basis. At first, they were a surprise and offered comfort. A feeling that he was still with her, living in the house somehow. Then, she found herself looking for them, anticipating them, and when she thought she'd found them all, she had experienced a new devastation.

"Is that Mr. Oliphant's writing?"

Mildred handed the note back to Carol for her to examine. She watched how tenderly the girl held it. Until now, no one else had ever known about Willis's notes, let alone read one. It had been something private between just the two of them. Mildred felt happy that someone else knew about Willis's notes, that they would live longer than either of them now.

"What's the S mean?" Carol looked at Mildred, her eyes bright with curiosity.

"His middle name was Sycamore," said Mildred. "I used to tease him about it."

"Like the tree?" Carol looked out at the old sycamore in the backyard. Its trunk had shed so many layers that it almost matched the bone white color of its upper branches.

"Like the tree."

Mildred shook her head as she pulled into the cemetery's entrance. She momentarily wondered where she had put that note and thought to look for it once she returned home.

Just before the path curved to the left and descended toward Willis's plot, Mildred slowed to a stop. The roadway was torn up, and a large barrier had been placed across its narrow width. She pulled the car to the side and took the flowers from the passenger seat. She walked to the barrier and looked beyond it, trying to decide if she felt stable enough to walk the path herself. She had no idea how she could get back up that incline, though.

"Excuse me, ma'am?"

Mildred turned to find a young man wearing the dark green polo that all the cemetery staffers wore. A golden outline of two birds in flight sat stitched near the top of his left shoulder.

"Can I help you get somewhere?" The young man's face was warm and inviting and offered no feelings of intrusion. The perfect makeup for this type of setting, Mildred thought.

"I'm just here to visit my husband," she said, cradling the flowers. "I typically drive right down this path, but I'm afraid I'll have to walk it this time." Mildred looked down the path again, convinced now she couldn't do it.

"May I ask who you're visiting to see if we can find you another route?" He pulled a small tablet from his back pocket and swiped its screen, ready to input a name.

Mildred told him Willis' name and the young man typed it in. She watched his face flush as the information popped up on his screen.

"Are you Mrs. Oliphant?"

"I am," she replied, uncertain of what the issue might be. The young man looked excited, and that confused her even more.

"Mrs. Oliphant, would you mind walking a few steps over here with me? I'd like you to look at something."

She consented and reached for the hand he offered to help steady herself. He led her to the grassy edge of the roadway that overlooked a whole field of plots, in the middle of which was Willis and his white flag. Mildred noticed several of the cemetery's yard crew scattered about the field. There were about four pairs of workers at different areas of the field. One would remove the existing flowers or plants at a headstone then place them on a rolling cart, and the other would make a note on a clipboard. Mildred thought it odd, but when she looked at her companion for clarification, he only smiled at her and encouraged her to look again. At the base of the field, Mildred saw an older gentleman in a dark green polo pulling a rolling cart full of red flowers. The gentleman stopped and retrieved a bundle from the cart then placed it in front of the headstone. He moved on to the next plot and did the same. Mildred scanned behind the gentleman to see where else he had placed the red flowers, and as the entirety of the field came into focus, Mildred had trouble catching her breath.

"Oh," she said. "Oh, my." Mildred tightened her grip on the young man's hand.

"You're a little early," he said. "We like to have this all done before you get here."

Mildred widened her eyes. "You mean you've done this before?"

"Every year, ma'am." He smiled at her. "Those were our instructions."

Mildred laughed out loud. First one burst of sound, then another. She leaned into him then looked back at the field once more. They stood there for a few moments, silent and happy. She thanked the young man and told him she'd come to visit another time. Once the path was fixed perhaps, which he promised would be very soon. He offered to take her a different way on one of their golf carts, but she politely declined, saying she had gotten all she needed from today's visit. Plus, she had a luncheon to get to, and her bridge ladies might appreciate some fresh flowers for their centerpiece.

As she drove away, Mildred smiled, staring at the giant S-shape of red flowers in her rearview mirror.

THE SHRUG

Sara Van Beckum

They met in a nude drawing class in the city. Meredith pegged Pete – the only guy in the class – for a sleaze right away. She knew the type. Or thought she did. She watched him carefully when the male model emerged from behind the curtain. She sensed no disappointment in Pete and instead noted how he interrogated the model's body, his chin in his hand for a long time before going to the paper with his pencil. Maybe he's gay, Meredith thought to herself. Maybe they could be friends. She didn't have any gay friends.

She sat beside him the following Sunday. He helped her with her spilled coffee the Sunday after that. She asked him to get a drink the Sunday next. And somewhere within that series of Sundays, Meredith started hoping Pete would try to kiss her.

Meredith went to a boutique in the Village that one of the younger teachers at school had mentioned in passing. It was a place she wouldn't have been caught dead in before a date with Pete loomed on the horizon. She lapped the store without even stopping at a rack. She didn't have to look at a tag to know the clothes were too expensive. The collection was so curated – only a handful of items. What was she doing here? How silly she had been to come. There wouldn't be anything for her here.

Then she saw it. Not on a rack, but on the young saleswoman steaming a dress behind the counter. A midnight blue silk shirt with little moons in their varying lunar phases. It was something Meredith wouldn't have looked at twice, but the prospect of Pete seeing her in it changed her into someone who would wear it. Who was this guy who could make her want to buy a top patterned with tiny celestial bodies that waxed and waned?

The surface differences between Meredith and the saleswoman – Meredith, tall, thin, reserved; and the saleswoman, short, shapely, and pert – made it particularly painful for Meredith to ask but she felt compelled. She had gotten this far.

"Do you have any more of those?" Meredith's voice came out sharp, startling both of them.

The steamer gurgled in the awkward silence that followed.

"The shirt you're wearing, I mean," Meredith said, her voice softer now.

"Oh, this?" The saleswoman set down the steamer and picked up the fabric at her waist. "Isn't this just the best? The little moons?"

Meredith couldn't find it in herself to agree because agreeing meant that the two of them had something in common and she felt so different from this young woman. From most women. Maybe from all women. And yet the saleswoman was right, those little moons, that night sky shirt *was* the best.

"Do you have any more?" Meredith asked again, her voice measured.

The saleswoman shot up an index finger. "We just might. Can you wait one sec?"

"I think I have one sec," Meredith said, regretting her tone at the same time she struck it.

The saleswoman investigated Meredith's face, trying to detect her meaning.

"I'm kidding!" said Meredith, striving for an air of light-heartedness. "Of course I can wait."

"I'll be right back," said the saleswoman. A layer of condescension now covered her default setting of cheer. She wandered into the black hole at the back of the store. Meredith stood at the counter, working her tongue over a poppy seed from her morning bagel lodged between two back teeth.

It seemed like a long wait, and she was considering walking out when she heard the high-heeled steps of the saleswoman re-approaching. Meredith neutralized her expression before turning to see the young woman trailing the moon shirt on a hanger over her shoulder.

"You're in luck!" The cheer had returned to the saleswoman's voice as if she had given herself a pep talk in the back. She extended the shirt to Meredith. "It's a 4."

"Look at that," said Meredith, doing her best to play along. She purposely bought clothes online to avoid interactions like these.

Meredith forced a smile and took the hanger from the saleswoman's outstretched arm. She was normally a size 6. Could she fit into a 4? With her free hand, she stroked the texture of the fabric. The cottony-silk slipped over her fingertips. She imagined Pete's fingers touching it. And her, underneath.

"I'll take it," Meredith said, surprising herself. She hadn't even looked at the price tag.

The saleswoman tilted her head ever so slightly and assessed Meredith with a quick and well-practiced survey from head to foot. "Do you want to try it on first?"

Meredith couldn't imagine prolonging this episode by trying it on. Besides she would make it fit. She had to have it.

"It's for my sister," Meredith blurted the lie out of nowhere.

"Oh, I love sisters!" The saleswoman bounced on her toes.

Just say *me too*, Meredith thought to herself. But she couldn't. Instead, she lifted her eyebrows and pinched a smile.

The saleswoman folded the blouse into tissue paper and inserted the package into a small lavender bag. She took the handle and presented it to Meredith. "My sister and I are really different too," she said.

The words *"I bet I'd like your sister"* rolled around in Meredith's brain as she took the bag. She faked a cough, covered her mouth in apology, and walked out.

On the subway, safely cloaked in anonymity, Meredith felt around the bottom of the bag to retrieve the receipt. $249. Her stomach dropped. She had never spent that much money on any material thing in her life. Who was this man that could make her do something so foolish?

She folded a sharp crease into the receipt and tucked it into the bag. The back of her hand brushed against the silk of the shirt, and it instantly soothed her.

It was thoughtful of Pete to suggest a restaurant in Hoboken. When he had said over the phone that he had made a reservation at Blue Eyes, Meredith had laughed, thinking Pete was making a joke.

There was a silence from Pete in which Meredith realized he wasn't.

"Is that the Frank Sinatra-themed restaurant down by the water?" Meredith asked, buying time.

"Have you been?" Pete sounded disappointed that it wouldn't be her first time there.

And in that split second, Meredith decided to just let it be, to shelve that version of herself for a time.

"I've never been," she said. "Let's try it."

The drawing class was over now, and since they had become accustomed to seeing one another on Sundays, it felt appropriate when Pete had suggested a Sunday. The reservation was for 5 pm – early for a date. And that hour on a Sunday felt more like the time reserved for a family dinner. But in both a strange and comforting way, it seemed natural to Meredith. It was as if Pete was already her family.

That day Meredith waited as long as she could to take a shower. When she finally did and with the date still three hours away, she washed each part of her body as if preparing for some kind of a ritual. She felt more kindness towards herself than she was used to. Almost as if she were seeing her body and its various parts through the eyes of a dear friend.

Afterward, she graded papers in her robe at the kitchen table. At 4 pm she slipped into the moon shirt, paired it with blue jeans to tone down the formality. The silk shirt wrapped around her like a hug. Yes, the size 4 was tight, but honestly, it pulled in just the right place, enough to give her a hint of cleavage. Something she usually judged other women for showing but now she wondered why she had waited so long to flaunt her own. The shirt had a kind of Cinderella effect on Meredith and made her feel like someone who could actually enjoy a date. In the past, she couldn't get past the treacly feeling of it all and had done nothing to find love. Her last glimpse at something close to it had been with her college boyfriend. There had been no dating, no courting in that relationship. It was a series of drunken hookups that had become a three-year relationship. When she caught him cheating on her, ending it had been nothing but a relief.

Meredith zipped up her leather jacket and floated down the stairs of her apartment building and out to the sidewalk. She lived just blocks from Blue Eyes. She practiced a saunter down

Willow Avenue but was still careful to avoid the cracks and imperfections in the cement. It was April, and the spring blossoms seemed to pop out on the trees like kernels of corn as she passed underneath. The sun had warmed the day but the wind whipped. A stray palm frond blew into her path. Must be one of those holy days for the Catholics, Meredith thought, as she eyed the Our Lady of Grace Church not far off in the distance. She picked up the frond and coiled it around her wrist as she walked.

Meredith took a breath before pulling open the heavy wooden door of the restaurant.

The nearly empty dining room had just reopened for dinner. Over the sound system, Sinatra sang about how Chicago was his kind of town. A busboy filled glasses with ice water. A waitress clinked silverware, rolling it into napkins over a white tablecloth.

There was Pete. His long-limbed runner's body leaned across the bar in conversation with the wizened-looking bartender as if he already knew him. From where she stood, Meredith could see the undefended expression on Pete's boyish face. He was open and curious. Still innocent. Somehow unhurt by the world. Or if he had been hurt, he had found a way to take it in stride. His dark hair had hints of premature grey over the ears, which played nicely against his otherwise youthful appearance. He had these subtle hollows in his cheeks. Twin locations Meredith already longed to run her lips across.

The door behind Meredith reached its close with a sudden gust of wind and an accompanying bang. Pete turned to look. His face lit up, and he waved to her even though she was only a short distance away.

"Meredith! Over here!"

Meredith brushed the palm bracelet off her wrist into her purse and stepped down into the bar area. Pete held his hand out for hers. She took it. He had a warm, strong grip. It calmed her.

"This is her!" Pete announced to the bartender. Meredith heard the incorrect grammar but also understood that this meant Pete had told the bartender about her. How had he described her, she wondered?

Meredith touched the silk of her shirt for a shot of confidence. She pointed at Pete and raised her eyebrow at the bartender. "And that's him!" she said.

Pete tucked his head and lifted his shoulders in a shrug.

"I guess this is us!" he said.

The bartender, whose occupation naturally included the regular witnessing of a romance in bloom, grinned like a good sport. "Welcome to Blue Eyes!" he said in a deep baritone.

Pete took Meredith's hand and pulled her in close. He smelled like licorice and fresh cut grass. Meredith let herself melt into him and the warmth of his body that emanated through the open-heart shape of his button-down shirt.

"Any chance you guys have a table that would allow us to stay right here like this?" Pete asked the bartender, and then he winked at Meredith. He actually winked at her. And darned if her mouth didn't slide into a smile.

Still newly dating, Pete got sick with a bad cold. Meredith came over with Sprite and saltines and orange juice and tiny pasta in the shape of alphabet letters that she heated up with a can of chicken broth. She spelled out "Buh-bye cold" with the miniature letters in an arc over the soup bowl.

Pete traipsed out of his bedroom, his quilt shrouding his shoulders like he was some kind of a wizard. He stopped when he saw what Meredith had laid out for him on the table. She attempted to wipe clean her expression. She didn't want him to see her amused expectation displayed so openly. Too late.

"Awww, you're sweet, aren't you, Meredith?" said Pete.

Meredith fumbled with the loose end of the saltine sleeve. "I am not sweet, Pete."

"And now you're calling me 'Sweet Pete'?" He teased.

Meredith rolled her eyes but couldn't hide the smile that welled up from an old place inside. She was a kid again, standing there in front of him.

"Eat your soup, Sweet Pete," she said, and she swatted at him with the kitchen towel.

When Meredith brought Pete home to St. Louis, she couldn't wait for her father to see how well he treated her. The first morning at breakfast Pete asked her mother if he could put on the kettle.

Meredith noted the raise of her father's eyebrow.

"Why, of course, Pete," said her mother. "A tea drinker huh?"

Pete's shrug was almost imperceptible. "Nope," he said. He winked at Meredith and reached into the front pocket of his jeans to produce a tea bag. "Lemon Zinger for the Zinger."

Meredith's mom laughed. "Look at that," she said.

Her dad snorted. "She's a Zinger alright."

Meredith caught Pete's eye and slashed a finger across her throat. She watched his smile fade.

The next time she visited her parents she happened to be solo. It was then she overheard her father say to her mother, "No Mrs. Pete this time, huh?"

When Meredith discovered where Pete parked his car on Willow Street, she would go out of her way to pedal past it on her way home from school. Her breath would catch every time she saw that rig of his. The International Harvester Scout. "Sounds more like a tractor than a car," she had said when he first told her about it. Pete had flown all the way to Colorado to pick it up. It was old school. White with wood-grain siding. Leaning a little. Stoic somehow. And his Scout there, against the curb, unmoving but full of potential, would wash a kind of contentment over her.

Meredith's next thought was a repetitive one. It was a thought she had shared with Pete numerous times. With a car like that, did he really need a vanity license plate? She flashed back to their initial conversation about it.

"Pete, 'Wranglr'? Really?"

"What's wrong with it? I fish."

"Yeah, but do you want to tell everybody you fish? And how often do you 'wrangle' a fish? When I hear 'wrangler,' I think Levi's. Most people will just think you're crazy about your jeans."

Pete shrugged. The guy had a language of them. And this one meant he wasn't going to get into it with her.

"I already ordered the plate anyway," he said.

She wanted to tell him that using "anyway" in this instance was grammatically incorrect, but she took the high road and even suppressed the sigh.

Meredith spent hours on Amazon ordering books about Paris the night Pete's parents called with the invitation. Hemingway and Stein, along with Rick Steves and Fodors. Probably blew half a paycheck on them. She had never been to Paris. Before Pete, she had always thought of it as a place for lovers and why go when you're not in love. But then when Pete had suggested it for their first anniversary, she had rolled her eyes and said, "Can you think of anything more cliché?"

She remembered he had gone back to reading the newspaper, his favorite pastime. Cover to cover. Daily. When she asked him about the habit, he had said he liked reading about change better than effecting it.

"You pick where we go then," Pete said from behind the Sunday Review. Meredith didn't say anything. Instead, she attempted to bore a hole through the paper with her stare. The paper rustled between them – a movement she understood to be a consequence of Pete's shrug.

Pete didn't engage in the battles she waged. It was the reason they had stayed together so long. He used to make suggestions, but over time, he began just to let Meredith decide everything. She kept wishing he'd suggest Paris again, but he never did.

Now, two years later, his parents had. Springtime in Paris. A family trip. How could they say no, she had said to Pete. He looked at her like she had two heads when she said that. She caught herself shrugging back at him.

Christmas morning, that same year. A big white box with a red bow under the tree. Meredith had rolled her eyes when she saw it. What was in there, a puppy? She did feel the briefest wave of excitement at the idea before pushing the thought out of her mind.

"Hold up," said Pete. He crouched behind the easy chair to plug in the string of Christmas lights. "Okay," he said. "Now open it."

The gift looked expensive. Meredith pulled at the end of the red silk ribbon, which she imagined had been expertly tied by the shopkeeper. It slid like lingerie off the shiny white cardboard box.

"Aren't you gonna guess?" said Pete.

"A new car!" Meredith said like a game show host.

Pete shrugged his maybe with an accompanying smile. The teakettle whistled.

"Freeze!" said Pete. "Lemme get the tea."

Pete went to the kitchen. Meredith looked over at her pile of exquisitely wrapped gifts for him. A new tackle box. A power vac for his Scout. A book about Lincoln. A short stack of Moleskines tied up with twine for the king of lists. And the one she was most excited for him to open – the map of upstate New York. Her way of saying, "Okay, let's go look for that house."

Meredith stroked the smooth sides of the unopened box. She admired its clean, sharp corners. She didn't even need to open it. And there was the tea coming. Pete's excitement. The wrapped map of upstate at the top of his pile. At that moment, she realized she felt something like happiness.

Pete returned and set the two cups of steaming tea down. He rubbed his palms together and dropped to the floor, cross-legged in front of her.

Meredith pulled off the top of the box. Suction, slight screech of the corners. Tissue paper on top. White. She reached down to the bottom layer of crinkle and felt the softest thing there. It was so soft that she thought for a minute maybe it was a puppy after all. She looked up at Pete. "What in the—?"

He smiled and shrugged. The slow, deliberate shrug that said anything's possible.

Maybe anything *was* possible, Meredith thought to herself before she pulled the thing out of the tissue. It came out like an accordion. A long length of fur. In the loveliest rose petal pink. Meredith held it flat on the two palms of her hands like a tray.

A beatific smile beamed on Pete's face. He bunched his shoulders to his ears and held them there, suspended. A shrug of pride.

Meredith heard herself say what she said next as if someone else had said it. She would recount the moment again and again.

She would wish she had draped the fur around her shoulders and said, "Oh Pete, I love it. I love you!"

Instead, she said, "You know how I feel about fur."

And with that, the gloss of the morning fell away.

Pete cocked his head at her, waiting for her to say something else. When she didn't – when she couldn't – he got up and left the room.

Meredith went to Pete's pile of presents and removed the wrapped map of Upstate New York. She tucked it behind a row of history books in the bookcase.

Not long afterward, they went on a two-day trip to the beach to have sex. Meredith couldn't do it in their apartment anymore. Something about the dog watching, she said. (Meredith hadn't been able to forget the possibility of a puppy inside the Christmas box. And the acquisition of Shirley from Accounting – Pete's jokey name for the dog that stuck – had become the not so subtle test for whether or not they could raise children together down the road. The test wasn't going well. Meredith was the Alpha, and Pete just shrugged when Shirl looked up at him.)

They stopped at a roadside stand. Pete had a burger. Meredith ordered a salad she didn't eat and french fries.

Pete told her about his demotion at work.

"When did that happen?" Meredith spat out the words.

"About a month ago, I guess?" Pete shimmied a fry from the pile on her plate, swung it through a lake of ketchup.

Meredith raised the globe of the plastic wine glass. "*Why* did that happen?" She scooted the paper plate away from her. Pete pulled it closer to him, staked another fry.

He shrugged his quick isn't-it-obvious shrug. "Manny thinks I'd be a better team member I guess."

"Who goes from team manager to team member?" Meredith asked not Pete, but the meniscus of the bad Chardonnay as she teetered her glass back and forth.

Pete crept a smile and performed a slow raise of his hand. When Meredith didn't laugh, he took a long sip of his beer.

The sex that afternoon veered into rough territory. Pete didn't like it, but Meredith insisted. "Handle me," she said. "Just fucking handle me." She took his hand and slapped it hard against the back of her leg.

That morning. The morning. An otherwise ordinary day. The trip to Paris with his parents still weeks away. The two of them in a new stage of bickering. Pete proving himself a worthy sparring partner at last. This one started with the origin of April Fool's Day. Then about what the "D" in D-Day meant. It spooled from there. Whose idea it was to say yes to a friend's brunch invitation. How Pete's friend Jordy had or had not hit on Meredith's friend Lisa. Who took the garbage out last. Whether to offer her mother their bed when she visited. (Meredith said no, Pete said yes.) Buying versus renting. How to spell *eviscerate*. The Catholic Church. The cable bill.

One of those. Or none of those. Or all of those.

Afterward, when Pete came out of the bathroom where he had stayed for a very long time, Meredith was brushing the dog at one end of the sofa. Shirl bowed her head each time Meredith landed the brush on her neck before pressing down and snaking it the length of her long dachshund body.

"So what do you think we should do?" Meredith asked Pete.

Pete dropped onto the other end of the sofa, bouncing the cushion and Meredith and Shirl on it like a chain reaction teeter-totter.

"About what?" he said, loosening the laces on his Asics.

"Just what do you think? You're always reading the op-ed page, but you never offer any opinions yourself."

"Okay." Pete pulled up the tongue of his sneaker and inserted a foot. "I think it's complicated."

"You think what's complicated? Be specific." Meredith set the brush on the end table and used her hand to pet the dog.

"Everything. All of it." Pete tightened his laces.

"That narrows it down." Meredith rolled her eyes at the back of the dog's head.

"Well then, I'll put it back on you," said Pete. "What do you think?"

Meredith pushed Shirl off her lap. Plucked at her jeans, removing strands of dog hair. She wanted to show Pete how to be decisive. This. This is how you do it.

"I think we should split up," said Meredith. And she rubbed the tips of her fingers back and forth, strands of hair falling to the floor.

Pete paused for the briefest of moments. He tied the laces of his shoes. "I'm gonna go for a run."

"That's it? That's all you're going to say?"

"What am I supposed to say?" He held her gaze for a moment longer than usual, and she thought there was hope he would fight her on this. Don't let it end this way, she thought. She couldn't get herself to say it out loud.

"Have you seen my headphones?" asked Pete.

Without waiting for an answer, Pete opened the door and walked out.

"C'mon Pete. You always liked being cutting edge," said Meredith. It was a barb, but even the barbs were coming out different since they had made the decision. Or since Meredith had made a suggestion and Pete went along with it.

"I'll think about it," said Pete. He was flipping through the stack of vinyls with his index finger. He paused at Led Zeppelin. "Yours?" he pointed at the cover, raised his eyebrows at her.

"What do you think?" said Meredith from her perch on the sofa. She was knitting; Shirl tucked in at her side.

Pete placed the album on her pile. Their stacks were almost even; their collection mostly doubles.

"We already told your parents yes. We bought the tickets. I've done all the research," Meredith went on. "Besides, do you really want to go to France without me?"

"We're planning to do everything without each other, Mare. Don't you think we should start now?"

Pete laid the Sinatra on his stack. Meredith dropped her knitting to grab for it.

"Look at the name. Top right." Pete said.

"Will you ever listen to this again?"

Pete shrugged. "You'll never know."

He had said it with a smile, but like most things they said to each other that had meanings they didn't intend, the words floated into the space between them and echoed loudly, percussed by the clicking of Meredith's needles.

Usually, Meredith only allowed herself a chair massage. In a nail salon. Ten minutes, ten dollars. But after the breakup, she paid for the real deal. The masseuse covered Meredith with a sheet and pressed her all over. The pressing felt like an assurance that she still existed. Made of something besides regret. Why wasn't this part of making love, she wondered? And what was it about this table that felt better than any bed she remembered sleeping in? Her body disappeared again the moment the masseuse took his hands off her.

The hour-long massage felt like it lasted five minutes. Or worse, like it had never happened. What kind of a bastard was time anyway? (She thought she sounded like Pete now.) Meredith sat in a café for a long while after the massage and thought about time. How five minutes could be infernal, say, to a child in church. Or waiting for your father to say something in the car that wouldn't make you cry. But an hour on the massage table felt like the time it takes to sneeze.

On her way home, she stopped at the deli. Seltzer water, a bruised banana, a KIND bar she bought for the name alone. Like unwrapping the words and eating its contents could remind her to be kind from the inside out. Sure, Pete was suffering too. Or so he had told her when they talked.

"How was Paris?" she had struggled to take the weight out of the question.

"I don't know, Mare, it was okay I guess?"

"Paris was *okay*?"

"What do you want me to say, Meredith?"

Meredith. Nobody who knew her – besides her father – called her that. And Pete? Pete hadn't called her that since their first night at Blue Eyes. He even introduced her as "Mare." He would say, "You know, like a horse." It would take people a minute, so Pete – every time – would finger-sketch a horse in the air. As if that would help.

She detected anger in his voice now. Another thing she wasn't used to hearing from Pete. She spun the ring on her finger that she had not yet been able to remove.

"Say something without a question mark at the end," she said.

She could swear she heard the slow, steady shrug Pete used for diffusing emotion over the phone. Sure enough, the anger was gone when he spoke again.

"This hurts like hell," he said. "But every day it hurts a little less I guess."

For Meredith, it was the opposite. Every day it seemed to hurt a little more. She felt like she was sinking in hurt. And dread. Dread that she would have to live with regret for the rest of her life. It was she who had made the suggestion that became the decision. There was no going back. Mostly because there had been no objection from Pete.

And what's more, she had noticed a kind of relief in him. His face, his posture, his whole mien had relaxed since that day. It felt as if Pete had found an upside to the break-up. And he couldn't hide it. It was clear to Meredith that he had a new-found hope about his future without her in it. She told her-self it was better this way for both of them. She couldn't bear to live through more ups and downs, beginnings and endings, hope that transmuted to dread. Better that Pete find someone designed for this kind of thing. Someone who imprinted less. Went with the flow. Took the bad with the good.

Meredith generally avoided Willow Street on the way to and from school now, but every once in a while, she would find her-self cutting the old path that would lead her by Pete's parked truck. Why not, she would think on these occasions. It can't hurt any more than it already does. The feeling she had when she saw the Scout was what she imagined it felt like to be a cut-ter. You make the slice, and the pain stops for a minute. Seeing the Scout kept Pete – and the pain of being without Pete – in her life. She considered herself broken up rather than alone. A cutout of Pete still lived with her. She made room for him in the apartment. She stayed on her side of the bed. Avoided his side of the couch. The few things of his she found, she left where they were. A pair of headphones, a couple of fishing lures, a shot glass from a wedding he was in, a nickel in the cleaned-out drawers of the bureau, a to-do list on the back of an envelope (haircut, ACE for nails, tickets to Springsteen, booze for poker).

The exception was the day she found his old running shoes tucked in a box with winter hats and gloves. She slipped her feet inside and flopped around the apartment until she tragically realized that she would rather his feet be the last to have worn them. She kicked off the shoes like there was a bug in them and placed them at the back of her closet.

It was April again – a whole year after the end that still felt like yesterday – and her mother was due to arrive for her annual visit. Meredith went to buy groceries to fill out the contents of her refrigerator. She usually looked forward to her mother's visits, but not this year. Her mother had loved Pete. Her father had even grown fond of him. To Meredith, it seemed both of her parents had come to prefer Pete over her.

Meredith slid a case of Diet Coke off a shelf. She swiped a bag of jellybeans from an Easter end-cap display and tore a hole in the top, popping the sugary ovals in her mouth as she steered her cart down aisle after aisle in a daze. In the produce section, she scanned the brightly colored shapes that just looked like toddler's toys to her. Pete had been the cook. She settled on the yellow bananas and the red tomatoes and the purply-blue eggplant.

When she got home, Meredith arranged the groceries in the fridge. Afterward, she made herself a cup of Lemon Zinger and took herself down to the storage cage in the building's basement. The dim light illuminated the still perfect white of the box. She pulled off the lid – its shriek bouncing off the cement walls – and lifted out the fur shrug. A yellow sticky note she hadn't noticed before dropped from the back of the fur and fell into her lap. She read Pete's printed square letters. "For You. In Paris."

Meredith nestled the shrug around her shoulders and rocked herself back and forth.

It was then she had the idea.

Pete had said yes right away.

"It's just, you know how my mom is about navigating her way here from the airport," Meredith said, even though he hadn't asked for an explanation. And what she said wasn't true. Her mother had always found her way to Hoboken all the years before there was a Pete and his Scout.

"No, I get it, Mare. Use the Scout. Pick her up."

"Really? You don't mind?"

"Not at all," said Pete.

They arranged for Meredith to get the Scout while Pete was at work. He would leave the keys on top of the back tire for her.

In bed that night, Meredith realized what had been so strange about their conversation. There had been no hesitation in Pete's voice. None of his familiar pauses. Could that mean he wanted to see her too? But then why would he leave the keys for her? Why wouldn't he make it so they would have to hand them off in person?

Meredith didn't know the answers, but the questions were enough to allow her to drift off to sleep on the wings of something that resembled hope.

Her mother stood waiting at the curb of the terminal; a lit cigarette dangled in her hand. It occurred to Meredith as she inched the Scout along in the slow-moving passenger pickup line that her mother looked like a smoking Queen Elizabeth. Tufts of graying hair poked out from beneath a headscarf patterned with cats and dogs. She wore short rubber rain boots and a long khaki trench coat that stopped just below her knees. One always knew the forecast when her mother was around. She was on a first name basis with the Weather Channel meteorologists and talked about them as if they were characters on a soap opera. *Would you believe Liane is pregnant AGAIN? Did you know Dr. Greg has a twin brother?*

Her smile, when she saw Meredith getting out of the parked car, was short-lived.

"You've lost weight," her mother said, as she pivoted the toe of her rain boot over her dropped cigarette. There was concern in her voice, tinged with a whiff of disdain. In their family, the women – Meredith, her mother, her aunts – were spindly. Weight was something they chased and held onto when they had it. Extra pounds meant there was a surplus of something. It was a sign of good health.

"I lost Pete," said Meredith, as she took the rolling red carry-on bag from her mother and heaved it through the open back window of the Scout. "He was a big weight."

"Meredith!" her mother said in a hushed whisper, turning her head to see if any passersby had heard.

"What, it's true!" Meredith said. "It's not like he died, Mom. Jeez."

She opened the car door for her mother and walked around to the driver's side. When she got in, she dropped her forehead against the steering wheel. Her mother placed a hand at the base of her neck but didn't say anything. Meredith hadn't expected to feel this rush of emotion. She had trained herself from an early age not to feel when she was around her family. But this was different. The swarm of rage, loss, embarrassment, frustration felt unavoidable. She wanted to pound her head against the steering wheel, but she just kept it there, unmoving.

There had been no note from Pete in the car. There was nothing at all left on which to hang a future with him. When she dropped the Scout off in an hour's time, that would be it. She was out of ideas. Out of time. She pressed her head harder to feel the metal of the wheel. Rather than crying, which she was often able to think herself out of doing, Meredith forced out a hard sound from the back of her throat.

"What is it, honey? Are you laughing?" her mother asked.

Meredith hauled her head up from the steering wheel and threw it back against the headrest, trying to catch her breath. She pointed at her mother's head.

"Those little cats and dogs on your scarf!" She put her hand on her stomach and laughed again.

"I thought you'd like those," said her mother, and laughed along with Meredith.

Meredith rubbed her forehead and then swiped the back of her hand over her eyes before turning the key in the ignition.

Meredith deposited her mother at the apartment then headed back to Pete's parking spot on Willow Street. She took the long way around, driving alongside the muddy green Hudson. It was still early, and only a few cars dotted the wide parking lot of Blue Eyes. I have five minutes to think, she told herself as she pulled into the lot. What would Pete do if the tables were turned, she wondered?

She wrestled the gearshift of the Scout into Park. She inhaled the vapory smell of diesel as she scanned the spare interior for a clue. Rifling around in the glove box, she rescued a pad of post-its. Pete, Mr. Post-it. Of course. One of her red correcting pens was there too. It was missing its cap, but a quick scratch against the pad proved it still worked.

"Pete," she wrote. "Thanks for the Scout. Also, I found some of your things at the apartment. If you want to pick them up, I'm around Sunday."

She leaned back and reread the note. Her breaths were coming in short and fast. Her whole body tingled. She angled the rearview mirror to see herself.

"What do you want?" she asked her reflection out loud.

There was only one way she could describe the expression she saw looking back at herself. She looked alive.

She shrugged at her reflection and went back to the note. At the bottom, she added a tiny shape of a horse with an M inside.

Back at Pete's parking spot, Meredith stuck the note to the leather patch in the center of the Scout's steering wheel. She rubbed the adhesive strip back and forth to ensure a good stick, placed the key back on the tire where she had found it, and walked up Willow Street, hoping.

SPRING GREEN, WI

Meg Cassidy

A sliver of new moon grows brighter as midnight closes in, turning silver to gold before my eyes. I struggle to keep them open as I wait up for Daisy, sipping one of Trevor's beers at the kitchen table. She's grown distant but will still spend the night with us most weekends. As usual, I try to stop myself from checking in on her like the nightgown-clad mother hen I've prematurely become—but easily convince myself that's exactly what she needs.

So, I text, *See you soon, sis?*, and wait there, nursing the lukewarm Miller Lite and staring at the same page of a paperback for almost an hour without a response before heading upstairs. Not wanting sleep so much as accepting that I need it. I wake with a start when Trevor comes in from his shift; it's 3:36 a.m., and although I see on my phone that she's responded, *Yep,* I tiptoe down the hall toward her room.

When I peek through the spare room keyhole and see her gangly, teenage legs spilling over the side of the air mattress, I can finally breathe.

The boys love having their aunt "Dizzy" over on the weekends. I don't know what we'd do without her since I work the weekend breakfast shifts, and Trevor lies dead to the world from his nights on call. T.J. and Will tell me she makes Mickey Mouse-shaped pancakes, letting them fill each big round ear with as many chocolate chips as can fit. My little sister, making me feel like crap for being the kind of mom that barely gets the toaster waffles warmed up before serving them on a paper towel.

Whenever I tease her that she's become more mom-like than me, she rolls her eyes and tells me for the umpteenth time she's, "never having kids, probably never even getting married, no offense." It rolls off her tongue like a mantra.

But I notice the changes, or should I say similarities, already starting to take root. Manifesting in new clothes, likely shoplifted from the strip mall just like I used to; drawing attention to her signature ponytail by sometimes tucking a daisy into it (ironically, or so she says); cartilage piercings, and probably a few tattoos I'll see once swimsuit season hits that convey she's starting to test the limits of her body with tiny doses of pain. It drives me crazy that even my thick-skinned sister isn't immune to the influence of those constant "smile, honey" voices that often feel ingrained in our DNA.

At 6:15 am, with my faded blue diner dress already slipped on like a second skin, I gently open the door to ask if she's okay staying with the boys again until Trevor wakes up. She murmurs yes, and I hesitate in the doorway wanting to go ask how her night was and pull the covers up more tightly. But she's already rolled over to face the wall, always one to resist affection. Even as a toddler she'd give obstinate little one-armed hugs, and Mom and I would tease her for playing hard to get—long before she knew what it meant. Daisy came off as aloof, but it was a trait I envied in her. From the day she learned to walk, it was as if she'd decided she was already done with this place and had somewhere better to be.

I blow a kiss to my sleeping boys, grab my stack of library books to return, and step out into the early morning sun to plow through another mindless day at the Hideaway.

I pass Mom's trailer park on my drive into town and make a mental note to ask Daisy for an update on whether the latest boyfriend (Chet, I think?) has moved in yet. Daisy and I were both born there, eleven winters apart. And with what I can only estimate was at least that many boyfriends in between, it's a wonder it's just the two of us: Carleen, a name that's always struck me as tailor-made for my waitress nametag, and Daisy, which could not have been any less fitting for her muddy, spitfire attitude. When we read *The Great Gatsby* in sophomore English, I remember rushing home to ask Mom if the glamorous Daisy Buchanan had been her inspiration for my then four-year-old sister. But a quizzical look was all I got for a reply. I stole my school copy (as I did with most books that resonated with me back then), and it became one of the only things Daisy would let me read to her at bedtime. When we're alone, I'll still sometimes refer to her as my "beautiful little fool."

Daisy got Mom's defiant streak while I was blessed with her passive-aggressiveness. With both of those traits rolled into the same person, we were never sure which side of Mom we'd cross paths with in the trailer's tiny living room. Any other differences Daisy and I had in our make-up, I have to chalk up to our fathers. I have only bad memories of Daisy's long-gone dad, and not a single one of my own, so the only commonality we have in the dad department is how we've acclimated to their absences.

"You got yourself a good man, Carleen," Mom still says proudly, at least every other time I see her. Like I've cured a disease or at least graduated with honors from some fancy school. Marrying a clean-cut, overprotective high school boyfriend while six months pregnant the summer after graduation hardly seems worthy of constant praise. But I can see how, to her, it might seem like I won the lottery with Trevor – a guy who takes solo cups out of my hand before I even get buzzed, who has a steady job and sticks around. I wonder if Mom says it more for Daisy to hear lately though. And I can't blame her for that. Daisy's already driving distances I don't even want to think about on dark country roads, shot-gunning beer with guys she meets online who live as far away as Minnesota.

I'm sure the last thing on Daisy's mind these days as her sophomore year comes to a close is finding herself a "good man." I hope, but simultaneously dread, that she's already starting to plan her great escape from Spring Green just as I was doing not *so* long ago. Although I didn't make it very far.

I park my minivan in the back lot of good old Hideaway-On-Main—my home away from home since I was old enough to pass for eighteen and serve drinks at the only diner/tavern within walking distance to the trailer park. Unless you count the gas station rest stop that provides both meals and showers for truck drivers and drifters. Mom is usually posted up there, chain-smoking and chain-dating with the same group of "gals," as she still calls them.

The Hideaway shares a parking lot with the Spring Green Public Library, and I slip most of my books through the returns slot, keeping one on me, as always, to occupy me between taking orders and wiping tables.

What I thought was phase one of my great escape has become my life. I spend more time at the Hideaway some days than I do at my own house. On Saturdays, it's just me and Kenny, the 60-something cook who is short on small talk but has shown me more kindness than anyone else who's ever stepped foot in here. The owners, a couple who have since moved a few towns away and operate similar dingy establishments scattered around the area, have no idea that every night, Kenny packs a full meal for me to take home to Trevor and the boys. He knows all their favorite sandwiches and always puts in veggie sides instead of fries, a two-dollar upcharge, which I convince myself makes up for all the grease that comes along with anything cooked on The Hideaway's ancient griddle.

Like everything else in the place, Kenny looks the same as the day I started working here when he taught me how to use the frozen custard machine, the longest conversation we've had to date. It's the same menu—both the food offerings and the sticky laminated menus themselves, same coffee maker spitting out sludge that tastes stale from the moment it's done brewing, same mildewed red and green plaid carpet, same neon beer signs that buzz annoyingly at night and keep sunlight from streaming in during the day. And same-ish me. Thanks to the large, rarely-washed windows at the front of the diner, I can see just enough of my blurry reflection that it's easy to pretend I'm still 15.

When I started working here, the job itself monotonous within the first week, my mind would run wild with thoughts of saving up for one-way tickets to California, college tuition, a tiny apartment of my own in a big city. I counted every penny, letting the same men we went to church with pinch my ass as they ordered lunch. It all seemed worth it to watch the measly tips add up. Trevor teased me that I'd amassed a small fortune when I told him how much was in my savings account, right before we drained it all on a modest wedding and baby furniture. These days, I slip into a dreamlike dullness as soon as I start setting the twelve sturdy wooden tables that look like they'll survive the apocalypse, then the ten seats at the L-shaped countertop, then refilling the S&Ps, and so on. I could run the place in my sleep, and on quiet Saturday mornings, it feels like I do. Serving up a few rounds of corned-beef hash and meatloaf in a fugue state to men who now treat me as indifferently as their own daughters. That part I'm grateful for. The tips were slightly higher when I started, sure, before they got used to seeing me in the same uniform, sometimes stretched over a pregnant belly, but I prefer their apathy. No jokes or wagers over my virginity as I walk away from card games, no phone numbers written in threatening scrawls on bar tabs. We've settled into a dysfunctional family dynamic I'll probably be a part of until this place shuts down.

It's fine, I convince myself when my girlhood daydreams creep back in. It's so easy to spend my days here. Keeps my boys fed. And what else would I do at the ripe old age of 26?

My biggest worry these days, is that Daisy won't get out. As messed up as it is, she's become my second chance. And I can't help but resent that our Mom didn't give me that same small courtesy. In all the parenting books I read, it seems like the pressures of having a helicopter parent badly backfire. But what about a helicopter sister? I wonder if that's why Daisy has been so reticent around me recently.

Saturdays are a drag without the promise of her coming in after school. On any given weekday, once the lunch crowd clears, and all the rusty Trump-stickered pickup trucks have driven away, I start getting excited – as excited as I used to feel waiting for a text from Trevor. I was shocked the first time Daisy and her friends came casually strolling in as if they were regulars. No one ever chose to hang out here when I was their age. I knew her girlfriends, had hosted many of them for sleepovers at my house, but standing there in my dull blue dress made me feel self-conscious in front of them. I could tell that I might as well be 50 in their eyes. Not that it made it any less tempting to pull up a chair and join them. Ron, the owner, once told me it was good for business to have "pretty young things behind the counter" so I'm sure he'd have no problem now with them loitering on the other side of it.

Within a week, I'd begun my afternoon ritual—with Kenny, of course, playing along—plying them with fried cheese curds, malts, and bottomless diet cokes. Heck, I'd pour them rail drinks if it meant they'd stay there all afternoon instead of venturing out to find trouble in neighboring towns.

On Saturdays like this, I realize how pathetic it is that just the promise of them coming in now defines my days. I stare back at my muted reflection in the window and tell myself, for the first time in years, that something has to change.

It's an unusually warm Saturday evening, and I'm careening down a narrow country road in the backseat of Mandy's car, sharing a spiked Snapple pink lemonade with Jocelyn, singing our lungs out to Rihanna. We're going to see what's happening at some guy's house a few towns away. Angie, the shyest among us, has been texting with him and begging us to go all week. But I had a hard time not just going to the Hideaway this afternoon, tempted to hang out there instead for an early bird special and head home for an early night with Carleen.

But my friends already give me enough shit for wanting to hang out at the diner on school nights. They'll never admit they love how we've claimed it as our spot, or that they're jealous they don't have a Carleen of their own, but I've known these girls since kindergarten, and the most important things between us go unsaid.

It's almost the end of the school year, and if we can't find something to stimulate ourselves as sophomores on the first warm weekend of the year, we're really headed down a dead-end street to Dullsville. So, I rally. Convince myself yet again that the boys a few counties over might just be more exciting. Laugh at Angie making a mess of re-applying her eyeliner as Mandy plows through potholes so big it feels like we're on a rollercoaster.

It's a far enough drive that we have to stop and put five more dollars in the gas tank. We won't think twice about showing up to hang out all night with random guys we've never met, but the thought of ending up stranded on the side of the road in these parts? Hell no. As we're waiting for Mandy to pay, I glance inside the brightly-lit BP station, see my brother in-law's profile, one person ahead of her at the register. I squint, my eyes suddenly blurry like they can't accept what I'm seeing. *What the fuck is he doing out here?* I think or possibly say out loud. I haven't had that much to drink yet, but suddenly I can't think straight.

Mandy gets back in the driver's seat, and I grab her arm. "Follow him. *Please.*" I say, pointing at Trevor's truck, which he's already gotten into. And although I want to look away, I can make out a woman who is definitely not my sister in the passenger seat.

Angie starts whining that we have somewhere to be, but Jocelyn silences her with a gentle shove to the shoulder.

We're back on the road, heading in the same direction, the radio turned off. It's barely dark enough to need headlights, and I can picture Carleen just tucking T.J. and Will into bed and finally sitting down for a few quiet hours with a book, waiting for me and this apparent asshole of a husband to come home safe and sound.

My heart pounds, adrenaline seducing me to take the wheel and use Mandy's crappy old Corolla to ram Trevor off the road so we can deal with this right here and now. Or just leave him in a ditch.

My friends are silent for a few miles, respectfully waiting for me to say something. But when it's clear I'm not going to, Jocelyn puts her hand on my knee and murmurs, "I'm sure it's nothing, Dizz."

Each tiny town we drive through feels like a minefield. I breathe a huge sigh of relief every time they don't stop somewhere, and then the anxiety hits even harder during the next dark stretch of highway.

How is this happening? My mind is combing through every interaction we've had since I was six, searching for signs of betrayal. Trevor wasn't ever very attentive to me, but that's how I thought most big brother figures were. Plus, I'm not easy to be attentive to. And compared to the men Mom brought around, Trevor was never someone I felt like I had to worry about. He and Carleen started dating soon after my dad moved out, and Mom nicknamed him the White Knight the very first time he came over for dinner. I sometimes complained he was too protective of Carleen, and in the past year, I tried telling her she deserved more nights to herself. But supposedly, he worked third shift as a small town first-responder.

When we finally see his turn signal, my heart skips a beat.

"Should I follow?" Mandy timidly asks. Jocelyn answers affirmatively for me, and we park in a far corner of a dive bar parking lot. The place doesn't look all that different from Hideaway except that it's literally in the middle of a cornfield, at least 30 miles from Spring Green.

The windows must be painted over with something because you can't see inside at all. Mandy offers to pay the bouncer, and we round up $17 in ones from our purses to help the cause, but she reappears less than two minutes later. We couldn't even get in if we had ten times that, she informs us.

I open a text and selfishly think about telling my sister that *I'm* in trouble. But what would I even say? And what if I told her the truth? *Hey, maybe come way out to this shitty bar on the corner of Hwy 21 and Junction B, I'm pretty sure Trev is here with another woman?* I think about calling, just to hear her voice, when I see them come out.

I know Trevor has a gun in his car for his weird job, and I picture him taking it out and putting a bullet through my head. But he's wrapped up in whoever the hell this is. I open my camera app, triple check that the flash is off, and silently hand it up to Angie in the front seat. She zooms in, professional paparazzi style, just as they start to make out.

I put my head between my knees, and finally say, "Let's go," after what feels like hours.

Nobody questions me, but after Angie hands my phone back, she rolls down her window, and way louder than I would've guessed she could scream, belts out "Fuuuuuuck youuuuuu, Trevor!" across the parking lot as we peel out, back onto the highway.

We're howling with laughter for about a mile until Mandy, coming up for air, asks if I still want to get dropped off at Carleen's house later tonight. And all of a sudden, I'm choking back tears.

The first time I suggested going to Hideaway-on-Main one random afternoon last fall, my friends thought I was kidding. "We'll get abducted!" Jocelyn shouted, flinging her arms wide as if that was the least of her concerns. But with nothing else to do and nowhere else to go, it quickly became our favorite destination.

"Club Hideaway tonight?" we'd say, passing in the hallway between classes. The popular guys in our grade did not get it and were always questioning what we were up to there.

"Why do you hang out in that crusty place all the time?"

"Looking for your sugar daddy again after school, Daisy?"

Sometimes they'd investigate in person for a while, but they couldn't break the magical bubble that Carleen created for us at her counter. It was clear they were nervous in her presence—her pretty features still youthful but carved out enough to intimidate even the boldest teenage boy, their vulgar mouths suddenly tight-lipped as soon as she made eye contact. They never stayed very long.

We, on the other hand, were the best customers by far (except for the fact that we rarely paid more than a tip and a joke to Kenny at the end of our stay). Carleen would chat with us just the right amount for hours on end—filling us in on town gossip she'd overheard from the lunch crowd, always noticing and complimenting new haircuts and earrings, joking about our poor prospects for homecoming dates. All that separated us was the two-foot countertop and just over a decade. Some days I had an overpowering desire to trade places, so she could just sit, and relax, and not worry so much.

I give her a hard time about being such a worrywart, but it's nice to know that someone will care if I'm there the next morning. Plus, Mom's latest boyfriend is one of the biggest bums yet. I hate sleeping there because he'll leave the trailer at all hours of the night —paying no attention to the slamming metal door— heading out sometimes in his truck, sometimes on foot, always taking his dogs along as if he might never come back.

When Carleen and Trevor moved into their five-bedroom farmhouse a few miles from town, I was nine and immediately claimed the first bedroom at the top of the stairs as my own. Mom and I both probably would've moved in if they'd let us. Trevor had just inherited it from his grandmother, and compared to our trailer it felt like a castle. Never mind that nothing had been updated or cared for in decades. Carleen's done a good job in the years since, clearing out all the moldy furniture it came with, but to the point where it's barely furnished now, especially upstairs. There's a bed or a crib in each room, an air mattress in mine, and Carleen uses the last one as her dressing room (although she always rolls her eyes when she calls it that). There are a few plastic hangers with the same limp, light blue waitress uniforms she's worn for as long as I can remember, and a few brightly colored dresses left over from high school that I'm sure still fit her but look so dated. The few times she's offered them to me and my friends, we've awkwardly insisted she should keep them "for if, um, a special occasion comes along."

In middle school, when the old house was still full of new adventures, Carleen would let me invite a few friends to sleep over. Sometimes a girlfriend or two of hers would join, and they'd make some weak cocktail, insisting that we split shots so that she could justify it. Her friends would impress mine with sexual stories better than anything in Cosmo while Carleen and I pretended to be grossed out. Trevor would always make himself scarce—either working third shift or heading to the Hideaway with his own high school crew.

Or so he said. I wonder now if that's when it began. Ever since they moved into that huge house, Carleen has seemed more strained than she ever did at our trailer or their previous little apartment in town where they first lived together when T. J. was born.

Whenever Mom is over, she goes on and on about how having such a big kitchen is every woman's dream and talks about all the fancy dishes she'd make there. But I've never even seen Carleen cook in it unless you count unloading the little Styrofoam boxes Kenny packs for her to bring home.

As Mandy drives, I torture myself over how, or if, to tell Carleen what we saw. It feels like I've been handed a blood money lottery ticket I now have to decide whether or not to cash in. More than making her sad, I worry that not getting any reaction would be worse. Best-case-scenario of showing her the pictures on my phone: Carleen flies through the house enraged, packing a suitcase for her and the boys, then drives us all far away.

But, instead, I show up like a ghost in the middle of the night and say nothing.

The next morning is a Sunday; I've been tossing and turning on the air mattress from the moment I laid down, so when I finally hear Carleen coming to tell me she's leaving for work, as she always does, it's a relief.

I roll away from her, tempted to ignore her just a little while longer, but something in me whispers *go*.

She's shut the door by the time I sit up, and I can hear her already back downstairs. Suddenly, I'm up and in the hallway. I pause at the top of the staircase before following her. Looking through the octagonal window at endless fields of baby corn stalks drenched in early morning sun, I gaze into the light a second too long and am momentarily blinded. I have to feel my way down the stairs toward the kitchen.

I blink a few times and can tell she's surprised to see me, even more so when I ask if I can go to the diner with her for the breakfast shift. "Trevor came home last night, right? So, he can stay with the boys?" She nods with narrowed eyes but still doesn't ask any questions. We drive in silence, past Mom's trailer, into the empty town. Sundays at Hideaway are always quiet until the after-church crowd arrives. Kenny brings us both a cup of freshly-brewed stale coffee, and I help Carleen set the tables and the countertop. Maybe I'll offer to take some shifts from her, so she can stay home with the boys more or maybe take a class at the junior college. Maybe I'll take the next ten years of shifts and convince myself that this is all we were born for.

I let myself daydream until I can feel Carleen's eyes on me. I can't leave her waiting in the dark any longer.

June

209

Myke Johns

209 remembered the day the Hargis couple moved in, the way Shelly had stepped into the middle of each room and looked up as if she were an actor finding her light. 209 remembered a party where someone accidentally threw a plate full of shrimp through the window above the kitchen sink and into the backyard. That was a good party. After that party, the detritus of celebration all around, Peter and Shelly lay on the living room floor, too exhausted to clean just yet, content to leave it until morning, content with each other. She told Peter she loved this house, her palms flat on the floor, her legs slowly kicking at the baseboards. The floor took in the warmth of her body, absorbed the blows of her feet. It held her words in the air before tucking them away into the beams of the ceiling. 209 wanted to reciprocate— it loved her, too—so 209 held Shelley as tenderly as one might cradle a newborn bird.

Peter and Shelly threw more parties. It was their first house—a place with a yard and multiple rooms for guests to congregate. They invited their friends over, and their friends invited friends and the house hummed with conversations. Peter kept the kitchen a constant swirl of hors d'oeuvres and liquor, or he'd man a small grill on the back porch next to a cooler full of beer. Shelly buzzed from joke to thoughtful one-on-one, and the windows sparkled and the walls flexed. Nearly every light was turned on and jolted the house like caffeine jitters. The plumbing flowed until the pipes sweated and as more bodies filled the space, the air conditioner took gulping breaths.

In the last hours of these parties, the crowd would dwindle, leaving the hosts in long, reflective conversation with the last three or four really good friends to stick around. Seated on patio chairs or around the bottle-strewn coffee table, 209 relished these moments, with their long shadows and laughter filling the place better than any crush of people could. Emboldened after a long night of absorbing conversation, 209 would attempt to interject, but the creaks and groans it knew to make were mistaken for "the house settling." Opinions went unheeded and observations unpondered as they were misinterpreted for the rattles of pipes and ducts. But 209 loved its inhabitants and forgave the language barrier. It loved them as a nurse loves an infant.

When the couple made love, they went into the bedroom and shut the door. This modesty created an intense cell at the center of the house. The dark of the room throbbed red and orange, and the walls inhaled as if porous. Air moved between shuddering floorboards like the diaphragm of a speaker playing a song too quietly. The overstuffed coat closet in the hall popped open, unable to strain against the down jackets and scarves any longer. The water heater clicked on and thrummed. The AC sighed into action, rustling the bed skirt and Shelly pulled the covers up over her as the chill hit her bare skin. Peter leaned into his wife and pulled her against his warm chest. The warmth radiated through the sheets of the bed, into the air and onto the walls. The house felt, in these moments when the bedroom door was closed and heat pressed on it like smoke, as if it were fulfilling a role greater than structure, more than shelter. The couple huddled together against the chill and felt secure in the soft darkness. There, the house recognized the elegance in small moves.

•   •   •   •

When a family moves into a house, there is a period of adjustment. Previously barren walls carry the weight of framed photographs or provide a backdrop for furniture new and old. Floorboards flex under new footsteps and electricity courses through the veins of the place at night. Inhabitants enliven a house.

209 King Street had never been anything before it was the Hargis family home. Shelly had by chance seen it being built and had made her husband go see about buying it. He'd done so dutifully and still seemed bemused nineteen months later as he sat at a table applying his signature to documents. She had not been wrong about it. There was room for the two of them to thrive and to grow. But it was not too large, this craftsman with the brick façade, inviting front porch, and the oak trunk pillar in the living room. There was room there for them to move freely on their own or, more frequently, as one.

It took longest to unpack the stuff in the kitchen—the thousand little things that belong there. Peter held her, and they looked at their home together, how they seemed to fit perfectly into it. Beneath them, the floor felt for the first time the attention Shelly Hargis had put into arranging the furniture there. The imbalance and heft of the move gave way to the ballast of well-thought-out interior design. There was an invisible symmetry in the way the refrigerator and the cabinets seemed to radiate around the butcher block island. And the floor was appreciative that it played on the strengths of the support beams so there was no vulnerable spot where a footstep could cause the china cabinet to sway and clatter.

And it was not just the one room, but entering the house felt like stepping into a river, naturally eddying from hallway to living room to bedroom to porch. And while Peter Hargis himself may never have noticed the way the mirror by the front door was arranged just so to catch the reflection of the birch just outside of the kitchen window, he still felt a sense of calm as he adjusted his tie in it every morning.

The final box of newspaper-wrapped cookware dispatched, Shelly danced to the living room and dropped onto the couch. Her husband followed behind, their shoulders nuzzling together as they leaned into each other side by side, admiring this home they had created. The floorboards beneath them gave slightly, flexing just so, sounding like the satisfying crack of a fistful of knuckles.

The Hargis couple's modesty created a life. Shelly had been dutifully making charts and marking a calendar and taking her temperature as if she were about to go on a deep-sea expedition. The morning she realized she was pregnant, she sat in their bathroom, Peter still asleep. She held the test in her hands, staring at the plus sign she'd put there. She was at once overjoyed and panicked and serene. Alone, a room away from Peter yet a thousand miles away, she felt a current of sadness. Shelly dipped herself into it and shuddered. The pregnancy test clattered to the floor as she gripped her face in both hands. Peter stirred at the moans but did not rise. Shelly hugged herself, wiped her face, and picked up the test. She called out to her husband.

Energy cannot be created or destroyed. Every word uttered goes somewhere—vibrations moving air and hitting walls, chopped up by ceiling fans. Blown out of windows. Years of words clung to 209 like cigarette smoke. If 209 had any capacity for memory, this was it—the tiny utterances still trapped in brick. While the Hargises slept in the calm quiet of night, 209 would sometimes extract words brushed beneath a sconce or tucked behind a vase, and relive the conversations once again.

One conversation, in particular, was sharp. The floorboards, the ceiling, the oak pillar in the living room had soaked it up like red wine splashed across a tablecloth. 209 had been fascinated by the energy of it all.

The Hargis couple had invited Peter's parents over. Shelly's lived in Connecticut and would pay a visit soon, but now Peter was taking his father's coat and hugging his mother, Shelly offering them wine and appetizers.

At the news, Peter's father leaped from his seat on the couch and hugged Shelly, his congratulations likewise bounding around the room. Peter's mother gave a tight, short hug and sat back down.

The aroma of cedar-cooked salmon, steamed asparagus, red potatoes seared with rosemary filled the dining room. The ding of silverware punctured good-natured conversation. Where Peter's mother sat pinched the floor—her upright posture forcing the front legs of her chair into the wood. The house snapped beneath her as she finished her second, then third glass of wine.

"Are you sure you want to keep this one?"

She had spoken casually as she lifted a glass of wine to her lips. The others stared at her as she swallowed.

"Mom!" Peter said, his fork hovered in mid-bite.

She raised her eyebrows and went back to her potatoes in reply. Shelly stood and nearly ran to the kitchen. Both Peter and his father glared at the woman at the table, but she was stone. Peter muttered something profane and followed Shelley to the kitchen.

"Honey..."

"I don't care," she had yelled, her words ringing off cabinet doors, amplified in the wine glasses in the dining room. "Just get them out of my house!"

●　　　●　　　●　　　●

There had been a baby before. Years ago. Shelly hated to think of it as an accident. Life deserves a better term than that. She and Peter had been living in a three bedroom apartment with three other people, all pooling their meager incomes to live in an ancient and failing house within walking distance of downtown. It was a fitfully exciting life tacked together with coffee shop tips and graphic design jobs. But the ill morning came when there was a test. Then another. Then a long quiet conversation on the end of their bed. The window unit rattled and sighed, fighting the hot June humidity outside. The noise was a welcome punctuation, making long pauses in conversation seem less excruciating. Shelly sat, she remembered, her elbows denting her knees as she leaned toward the floor. Peter—he was so good, even then—rubbed her back and assured her he would be there next to her the whole way, whatever they decided. She remembered sliding from his reach, standing straight and looking at him there on the bed.

"We can't have a baby."

Peter stood and faced her.

"We can't have a baby," he said. His expression was kind, firm, and he had that worried look he got when he was searching her for a pathway in.

"Later, but not now," she had said. The color had drained from both their faces—they could have blended into the white walls and become a part of the house and stayed there, silently observing those who would take their place, removed and serene. Shelly carried this fantasy to the doctor's office. She imagined she was a house, separate and distinct from the horror going on inside.

After the abortion, she had been restless and uncomfortable at home. The pallor of their room felt deathly. A place which was still abuzz with activity now felt gauzy and dead to her.

"We're still a family, the two of us. This place is alive as long as we're in it." Peter held her close, wishing kindness was enough to convince her, knowing it was not.

"How can a place be alive?"

"How can it be dead?"

Over two hundred and sixty loads of laundry passed and the humid June returned as Shelly's baby grew inside her. She took to lying supine on the living room couch, wearing boxers and a tank top and leaving her belly exposed to the room. 209 felt her comforting weight against its joists and made the ceiling fans spin a little faster, let the cold air flow through its ducts and billow into its rooms until Shelly was forced to go grab a blanket from the bed. 209 would feel her belly as she reached into the upper cabinets to get a glass, Shelly brushing against the countertop.

"Hartford?"

Peter nodded as Shelley stared at him, cautiously elated.

"Connecticut," he said. "It's not a promotion, exactly, but..."

"We'd be close to my mom." Shelly finished his sentence. "When?"

"Soon. We need to find you a doctor, and we need to find a new house."

These words, like all words, reverberated around 209, their waves deflecting and dissipating as they permeated the room. The house absorbed them uncomprehendingly.

Shelly began packing in earnest the next day. 209 noticed a newly uncomfortable heaviness in the kitchen as boxes of plates, utensils, crock pots, anything not of immediate need began to stack there. Now four months along and beginning to show, Shelly focused on small things, and on days alone at home would turn the stereo on and sing as she labeled boxes of clothes to donate to Goodwill. 209 only knew something was wrong. Shelly's wonderful voice filling its empty spaces, once its favorite sensation, now turned frightening. 209 began to feel hollowed out, Shelley carving the life from its every corner. The house grew stiff and tense.

Peter brought no comfort as he removed the boxes from their stacks on the floor. As the first of the furniture disappeared, 209 held its breath, and the house became terribly cold inside. The couple bundled up and began unplugging things. The electric meter slowed, and the house felt duller than it ever had. When the kitchen table was taken out, 209 could only recall the brilliance of large meals, the people gathered around. It remembered the angry conversation from months before, the smell of rosemary and the hot, airless tension and it understood this feeling. Staccato cracks rippled through the house. Water flushed hot through pipes until steam filled the attic.

Floorboards creaked resentfully as movers carried the sofa out to the van parked on the street. Shelly wrapped her arms around her as she wandered from room to emptying room. Each step across the cold floor sounded like bones snapping. She moved to the kitchen, walls groaning around her. Shelley ran water from the kitchen sink, splashing her face cool, holding her wet hands against her skin and running them through her hair. 209 ran cold. A chill shivered through the attic—ice water through hot pipes. Copper cracked, valves and fittings hissed and spat, and water hemorrhaged into the dark.

Water trickled down the walls in the front room. Before Peter could wonder *what the hell*, a river eddied from hallway to living room to bedroom and onto the front porch. A panic of footfalls beat against the timbers; all ran to the door except for Shelly. The rising flood strained against the attic floor, and the ceiling above her bowed and darkened. Both Shelly and 209 remembered their first day together, her centering herself in each room. Shelly stood against the oak pillar in the living room, her palms pressed against it like the figurehead of some ancient ship. She glimpsed herself in the mirror by the front door. The attic door burst open, and water gray with dust gushed throughout the house and surged around Shelly's ankles.

"I'm sorry," Shelly whispered. She stepped downstream into the frame of the front door. The house lurched sickeningly to the west and trembled for a moment. Shelly put her hand to the door frame, leaned over and kissed it. Then she stepped onto the front lawn, water roiling all around her, choking the grass, filling the street. There was a crack like thunder above them, and Shelly stood with Peter and watched the roof collapse.

For a brief moment, 209 felt the sun shine into its darkest places before its walls gave in, toppling to the ground and throwing dust like ghosts into the evening sky.

LAST JULY

Richard Etchison

D anny and his dad, Leland, stood in the humid morn- ing and stared at the Volkswagen van. It was a perfect sky-blue rectangle with a snub nose, engine in the rear, rusting tailpipe, and open blinds adorning all the windows. The duo climbed in and started the engine, which sounded more like a lawnmower than an automobile. Puttering northward on I-75 up the spine of Florida, Danny unfurled a crisp new U.S. roadmap, and asked, "Do you want to stay on the Interstates until we're out of Florida?"

Leland cleared his throat. "Yeah, I reckon so. We've seen everything interesting there is to see in Florida."

"Roger that. Then take this all the way to I-10 and head west." Danny thought for a moment. "Dad, I want to go see the Astrodome this year."

"Plot us a route," replied Leland, coughing quietly into his clenched fist.

"It's called the eighth wonder of the world." Danny flattened out a crease in the map. "What are the other seven?"

"I couldn't tell you. Some hanging gardens are one of them."

"I'll bet the pyramids in Egypt are one."

"I'll bet they are." Leland's cough deepened as he tried to catch his breath.

Danny turned on the radio and found some music. The tin- ny, static-ridden car radio accompanied Danny and Leland on every summer's trip, and this one was no different. Danny had plotted out this summer's itinerary in its entirety, Leland only holding the boy to one standard: the stopover points. Leland and Danny rarely spent an overnight in a motel or campground, since Leland had friends and family scattered all around the country. They had become infamous for showing up on doorsteps unannounced ready for a visit. Despite this, people were always pleased to see them.

On their first stopover at Roy and Valerie's up in the Virginia foothills of the Allegheny mountains, Leland strolled with Roy across their farm drinking beers and catching up while Danny played in the yard near the old three-story Victorian nestled under a thicket of red spruce. Roy was Leland's old Navy buddy from the war, and he always wore a mesh cap with a Navy World War II Pacific logo. They had known each other for over 30 years. The sprawling farm raised chickens, cows, pigs, and sheep – it was Danny's favorite place to visit on the summer sojourns. The house sat high on a hill at the end of a dirt driveway at the foot of a mountain, and Danny had become enamored with the cool mountains after always being in hot, flat Florida.

As the sun set, Danny smelled dinner cooking just inside the screen door. He was pretending to be a farmer as he enjoyed the sensation of the cool grass blades under his bare feet. He thought about what animals his farm would have and how he would work the tractor in the field until sunset and his pretty wife would be cooking dinner and tending to their two kids. Inside, Roy's mother, Valerie, cooked the best chocolate cake in the world every time they visited. Roy's two kids were all grown up and moved out, and Danny always slept in one of the kid's bedroom, the only boy's bedroom that looked like the boy still lived there, since there were model airplanes hanging on strings from the ceiling. Danny loved the creaky house, and he pretended he lived there. He planned on asking for a model airplane for Christmas that year.

The sun parried through the trees, casting shards of golden light onto the side of the house. Danny hopped into the tree swing and swayed back and forth, thinking about the girl he liked back at school. Her name was Holly, and she had sat with him at lunch twice. She would be a good farm wife, and they would sit on the porch together every evening, and smoke cigarettes like Roy and his mother did when the weather was good. Danny pretended Holly was there with him and took turns swinging.

Danny turned to find his dad was running at full speed across the field followed closely by Roy's bull. Roy wasn't far behind the two of them, making some sort of call to try and halt the bull's attack. The bull was gaining on Leland, and Danny ran toward them as fast as he could. The bull lowered his head, and at the last possible moment, Leland made it to the fence and yanked himself over.

"Dad!" Danny rushed over to Leland but quickly realized his dad was laughing. Roy caught up to them, catching his breath.

"Old John Bull don't like your father's attitude much, kiddo," said Roy.

"I will never be a matador," said Leland, who suddenly stopped laughing and started gasping for air.

Roy reached for him and turned to Danny. "Hurry and get your dad's inhaler, Danny."

The inhaler was always in Leland's little bag where he kept his pills and razor and toothbrush. Danny darted to the house and flung open the screen door. Up the stairs and into his dad's room. No bag! Into the bathroom, and found the bag on the sink. Danny rifled through the bag and pulled out the inhaler.

When he returned to the fence, Leland was not breathing so heavily, but still looked alarmed. He took the inhaler and breathed it in, held it, and breathed out.

"Good job, kid. Lucky you are a fast runner," said Roy, "You okay, buddy?"

Leland nodded yes, before coughing a bit. He put his arm around Danny and squeezed. "I'm okay now. It was an asthma attack. Go on and wash your hands for supper."

Danny walked back to the house, turning back to look at his dad every now and again. Danny's hands were still shaking. He wondered why his dad's coughing had gotten so bad lately. He had never had an attack like this one before. There were more pill bottles than usual in his dad's bag. Danny tried not to be scared by thinking of how much they were all laughing after Leland had jumped over that fence. Later, Leland, Roy, and Valerie sat on the porch smoking and chatting under the light of the porch light while Danny lay in the porch swing listening, trying to get the image of his dad gasping for air out of his head.

The VW van motored down the state road under the midday sun. It was a windy day, and Danny watched the clouds crawl across the sky. The air conditioner didn't really work, so they rode with the windows down. They headed into New England, bound for an uncle's house in Providence. Danny played with the CB radio unit that his dad loved to use to chat with truckers.

"Breaker 1-9. Breaker 1-9. This is Danny looking to take a 10-100."

"You got to use a handle. Not your real name."

"Oh. What's your handle, Dad?"

"It's 'Seventh Son.'"

"How come?"

"Because I was the seventh son in my family," explained Leland. Danny quickly calculated his uncles, and could only come up with four. Leland explained that two of his brothers had died, one when he was only an infant, and one of his brothers had died just last year. Leland's parents had also both passed on, and he had been widowed twice. Danny knew his dad was much older than his friends' dads. One time, Danny's Cub Scout leader referred to Leland as his "grandpa" which had annoyed both of them.

Danny tried remembering his mother, but couldn't recall much anymore, except that she had played tennis with him in the public park. Danny's friends had mothers, and they were very nice to him whenever he went over to play at their houses. But Danny felt frustrated that he could not conjure up more memories of his own mother. Her name was Eleanor, and every time Danny met a person named Eleanor or heard about someone named Eleanor, he thought of his mother. Looking up at the clouds that dappled the sky, Danny wondered if she was watching them.

"Breaker 1-9. Come in. There's a bear setting up a trap on road 83 in Connecticut. I still got to take a 10-100. Come on back."

Leland laughed. "If you have to take a leak, you don't have to announce it to all the truckers in New England."

Danny had never seen a dog so big. Herbert, an Irish wolfhound, came up to Danny's nose, and he belonged to the Isaacsons, Danny's mother's aunt and uncle. They had darker skin and hair like his mother had. Danny assumed they were rich since they lived in a big, fancy house with lots of vases you weren't supposed to touch and a big shiny piano in the living area that nobody ever played. Murray and Gayle were older than Leland,

and Gayle always hugged Danny and told him how proud she was of him or asked him how he was doing in school or what activities he liked to do.

Danny played fetch with Herbert in the backyard. The yard was cut so perfectly that it looked like a pro football field, and a high white fence enclosed the entire lawn. Inside the screened-in porch, Gayle was saying something to Leland and glancing at Danny, which made him feel self-conscious, so he stopped playing for a second. She looked upset, and Danny figured they were probably talking about his mother since Gayle had been her aunt. Then Gayle started crying, and Leland patted her shoulder. Murray stood nearby and glanced over at Danny. He wondered why they kept looking at him. Herbert sat next to Danny and whined. Danny assumed they were still reminiscing about his mom, but wasn't so sure. Leland's asthma attack flashed across his mind.

That night they all had supper at the fancy long table in the formal dining room, and Gayle and Murray asked Danny a lot of questions as they ate their corned beef. They marveled at Danny's ability to recite the times tables – he didn't confess that his dad had taught him them a long time ago while riding in the car one summer. Murray and Gayle kept telling him that he was special and very gifted. Later, in the living room, they were watching summer reruns when Murray came in and presented Leland with a cane that Murray said his father had used. Leland admired the dark red wood of the cane and let it rest against the arm of the couch. Danny fell asleep against his dad's shoulder wondering what use his dad would have for this cane.

The VW bus made its way westward per Danny's charted route, stopping to see Graceland, the St. Louis Arch, Mount Rushmore, and Devils Tower. They collected matchbooks from each attraction and threw them into the collection bag. Leland and Danny drove on Interstate 70 across endless prairie, the wind whistling through the windows, an Anne Murray hit on the radio.

"Look." Leland pointed to the horizon, where a line of towering peaks spiked out of the earth in a perfect line across the grasslands.

Danny leaned forward in his seat. He looked to his right and saw the line of mountains lasting forever. He looked left and saw the mountains going on just as long. Leland explained that volcanoes and earthquakes formed the mountains millions of years ago. Danny unfolded the map of the western United States and followed the line of the Rockies into Denver where they would have to travel over them.

"Will we see snow?" Danny asked, looking up from the map.

"I think so," said Leland, dabbing at his forehead with a handkerchief. "We'll go up Pike's Peak, and I'll bet there's some snow left from the winter."

Danny's heart rose in his chest when they finally got to the foot of the mountains. The Rockies were the biggest thing he had ever laid his eyes on, and he gazed at them without blinking, straining to see the snow-covered peaks. Hours later, Danny stood in some frosty leftover snow at the side of the road as Leland snapped a photo. When his dad moved the camera away from his face, Danny could see that he looked tired even though his smile was wide.

They stopped over near the top of Pikes Peak with a spectacular view of the Rockies. A breeze tickled the Aspen leaves above Danny as he bent over and tried to fashion his first snowball out of the slushy snow. He hurled one at his dad, who ducked while leaning on his cane.

"You want to see the peak, right?" Leland used the cane to help himself back to the van about 20 yards into the parking area. Danny watched his dad struggle for breath and asked if he felt okay. Leland explained that at high altitude there was less oxygen, but he'd be fine once they descended again. Danny hated seeing his dad use the cane but he seemed to need it now. It made him look like a frail old man. Danny had a vague fearful feeling that was getting harder and harder to shake.

The VW crept up the mountain road that snaked its way along the side of 14,000-foot Pike's Peak and snagged a souvenir matchbook once they arrived. That night Leland and Danny camped in the VW at the local campground. They spread out in sleeping bags on the bunks Leland had built on either side of the van. They cranked open the louver windows to allow the night air to stream in and move about the cabin. Leland had begun jewelry making as a hobby and was placing an Indian turquoise stone they purchased onto a silver necklace charm. Back home, Leland would sell various trinkets he had made at the local flea market on weekends. Danny pulled out the gold necklace that hung around his dad's neck.

"Do you ever take that off?"

Leland traced his fingers across the Star-of-David pendant. "It was your mom's," he said, tucking it back inside his shirt collar. "I only take it off if I go swimming in the ocean. Do you remember your mom wearing it?"

Danny squinted his eyes trying to conjure an image of his mother wearing the necklace. "I think so. What is it?"

"It's a Jewish star of David."

"Why did she wear it?"

"Mom was Jewish."

"She was?" Danny sat up and looked at his dad. "Are we Jewish?"

"You are Jewish because your mom was. I'm Lutheran because my parents were Lutheran."

Danny thought about that for a moment. "I'm Jewish?"

"Well, you can be anything you want, Danny. It's a personal thing, your relationship with God."

Danny looked out the window at the Milky Way covering the sky like a field of dandelions. Leland watched him closely, then unclasped the necklace.

"You want to wear it?" Leland placed it around Danny's neck and closed the clasp.

"It's yours though," Danny said, looking down at the pendant.

"What's mine is yours, Danny."

Once Leland and Danny crossed over the mountains into the city of Los Angeles, the air cooled suddenly. Every year, they stopped in Los Angeles, the city where Danny was born and where Leland and Eleanor had met. Grandpa Phillip was Danny's maternal grandfather and lived in a modest apartment in Culver City. Grandpa Phillip was a little bent over and smoked a pipe. He looked like a scientist with his distinguished round eyeglasses and full shock of graying hair. On a roll-top desk laid a stack of Danny's school papers and a framed school photo of Danny from last year.

"These are my homework papers, Grandpa. How did you get them?"

"Your dad's been sending me your school work for years. Your grandma used to love to see them. Are you still getting good marks?"

Danny nodded. Grandpa Phillip discussed all of Danny's scholarly strengths and weaknesses with him. He also showed Danny a photo album filled with tattered black and white photos of people from olden times, that grandpa explained were his Russian descendants. Apparently, his mom's family had to escape Russia in the 1800s. Danny found this endlessly fascinating and fell asleep curled up on his grandpa's brown tweed armchair very early that evening.

A hacking cough roused Danny awake. He sat up and smelled grandpa's pipe, and saw that Leland was smoking a pipe, too. The two men sat in the kitchen, talking in low tones.

"I don't think I could live in Florida," said Grandpa Phillip, "but I promise I will visit when I can get away."

"I just thought I would at least give you a choice," said Leland. "I guess there's not much room here."

Danny didn't fully understand what they were talking about, but the way their voices deepened and quieted, it scared him.

"I'm sorry I moved her way across the country so far from you guys," said Leland.

"Hey, you couldn't have known," said Phillip. "Truth is, Rose was pretty crestfallen and had some resentment, but what does it matter now?"

Danny couldn't sleep now, and his mind raced. He got up to make his way to the bathroom. His heart thumped. He wished there was a light on in the living room. It was too dark, and he couldn't see a thing.

By late July, Leland and Danny had made their way back east to southern Illinois, where the van purred down two-lane state roads through the small towns. They pulled into Danny's half-brother's driveway and stared at a home that looked as though it had been pieced together by a giant Lego set. His half-brother, Peter, had started with a modest two-bedroom house and built on several additions that didn't quite fit together. Peter was over 20 years older than Danny, so Danny felt Peter's kids were more like his brothers and sisters than his nephews and nieces. Peter and Linda were full siblings, and Linda lived in Florida near Danny and Leland. To Danny, who had no siblings his age, being engulfed by the tornado of Peter's three children was a shock to the system. They played and fought, ate lots of sugary snacks, and then played again. They enjoyed bringing Danny along for the ride.

For two weeks, they ran summer wild in the country town of a thousand people, fishing and bike riding and swimming and wiling away the interminable days. They ran through the village as if they owned it, going to little league games, hunting for crawdads, and shooting BB guns. Each day they returned in time for dinner caked in dirt and full of joy. Once they finished dinner, they went right back outside. Sometimes they camped in a tent in the yard. Sometimes they slept in a fort in the front room. Danny even fell in love again, with his niece Jenny's school friend named Lisa, but he didn't tell anybody. He thought about her anytime the noisy relatives didn't surround him and even stopped thinking about Holly back at home. Lisa was so sweet and pretty and nice with puppy brown eyes and pink cheeks and dimples. Every love song they listened to for the rest of the summer made him think of Lisa.

On the last night of the visit, Danny and Peter's kids played flashlight tag and caught lightning bugs. Danny overheard his father, Peter, and Peter's wife Sharon talking in the dining room when he came inside. He stopped to listen before rejoining the kids outside. They were seated around the table but not eating. It looked formal and cold and made Danny nervous, so he tried not to be detected.

"I don't know if Linda is going to go along with that," said Leland.

"Do we have room?" asked Sharon.

"Sure, we have room," said Peter. "Or we will. I'm building the sunroom as we speak."

"It would be a big change," said Leland.

"Change is good," said Peter. "Look, just let me talk to Linda. I don't want you worrying about this now, Dad."

"Truth is, son, I don't have a choice."

The table was silent for a moment.

Sharon finally spoke. "Why aren't you going to fight it, Leland?"

Danny didn't move a muscle. Something was really wrong.

"It's not worth it, honey. Trust me, I know," said Leland. "Wouldn't buy me much time anyhow."

One of the chairs scraped against the floor, and Danny panicked. He darted outside as quietly as possible. He didn't want to be scolded for spying. As he turned to close the door, he saw Peter leave the dining room and go upstairs.

Danny returned to the warm evening and grabbed his jar of flies. The three other kids were now all gazing at their jars full of lightning bugs.

"Let's let the bugs go," suggested Danny.

They carefully opened all four jars and watched the bugs fly back into the cooling air.

Danny continued. "I don't know if we should go in yet. They are talking real serious like someone's in trouble."

"It's about him." The eldest pointed at Danny, and the middle child smacked the back of her brother's head, giving him a look that told him to keep quiet.

Before they left the next day, Sharon gave all the kids haircuts in the kitchen, and then Peter gave Danny a ride on his motorcycle. Danny had asked for a ride every day since they arrived, and everyday Peter had told him he just wasn't ready. But after he and Leland had packed their stuff into the VW and were about to say their goodbyes, Peter asked Danny if he wanted to go for a ride.

"Hold on, little brother."

Danny held onto Peter's waist. Leland snapped a photograph of the two brothers on the bike. Danny's heart pounded in his chest as Peter revved up the engine. Leland smiled and winked at him as he stood with his cane in front of the VW. They went a hundred miles per hour, and the Star of David necklace fluttered in the wind, blown around to the back of his neck. Danny had never had so much fun in his life.

As they puttered down the highway into the stagnant hot Kentucky summer, Danny counted the matchbook collection. Caesar's Palace Vegas, 45. Golden Gate Bridge, 46. Lookout Mountain, 47. The collection was getting bigger since Leland no longer used the matches.

"This is going to be too many matches for the terrarium, Dad. We'll need a bigger one." Danny had a goal of collecting a thousand matches from different diners, national parks, and motels around the country. This year had been a watershed since they had traveled to Idaho and Montana, which had completed all 48 states in the contiguous United States for Danny's travels.

"Are we going to go to Alaska next year? I really want to go to Alaska and Hawaii so I can get all 50 states."

"Well, I'll see about installing some floats on the bus, so we can go to Hawaii," said Leland. He began to laugh, but it quickly segued into a coughing fit, gripping the steering wheel with one hand until he could find his breath again.

Danny handed him a tissue.

"Look at that," Leland said, pointing at a passing sign. "The speed limit is 70 in Kentucky. You want to go fast?"

Danny smiled, and Leland pressed the accelerator. The VW was slow to make it to 65, then 70.

"It's a new record," Leland said and winked at Danny.

Danny liked the different places they got to see. He liked the matchbooks, and visiting people, staying in different houses. He liked the different types of land: the mountains, the desert, the plains, and the woods. They had everything they needed in the van.

They rode in silence for a few minutes. Danny tossed the bag of matches into the back and began fiddling with the dashboard. Leland flipped off the radio.

"You know, you have a lot of people who love you. Did you ever notice?"

Danny looked over at Leland, sensing something in his father's voice. He hesitated before responding. "Yeah."

"You got Peter and his kids and Sharon. You got your Grandpa Phillip. He's so proud of you. And you got your great aunt Gayle and uncle Murray up in Rhode Island."

Hot tears stung Danny's eyes.

Leland continued. "You also got Linda and her daughters back home. She would do anything for you. You like her, don't you?"

"Sure," said Danny, dragging the back of his hand across his eyes.

"What is it, son?" Leland reached a hand over and cupped Danny's shoulder.

"What about you, Dad?" Danny couldn't stop his voice from cracking.

"What about me?"

"You said Linda and Peter and Grandpa Phillip and everybody. But you care about me too, don't you? You forgot to list yourself."

Leland pulled his hand away and regripped the steering wheel, looking straight ahead. "That goes without saying, Danny. That's just a given that I love you. No matter what."

Danny took a deep breath and reached for the map on the dashboard. He plotted out their route home. The route he chose would take them through quiet towns and hamlets, so it wasn't the fastest. It was okay, Danny thought. His dad would never know the difference.

THE MOTHERF*KING DUTCH

Tallie Gabriel

I t's been four months, and I still haven't gotten used to life here in heaven. I mean, I say "life," but…you know. Existence? Nonexistence? Whatever. Anyway, it's way different than I expected. Not that I can pin down what I was expecting, exactly…pearly gates, honestly. And, like, angels welcoming me with harp music. I'd never thought about it further than that. I didn't even know if I believed in heaven, really. And then there was always the question of whether or not I'd even get in. Ha. It sounds funny put that way like heaven was some top choice college or something. College… Sorry, Mom and Dad, you busted your asses to pay for my need to study archaeology at UCLA, and I went and got myself motherf*king killed ten days after graduation. Sorry about the swearing, too, but Mom you always said that curse words were okay when there weren't any other words that adequately expressed your emotions, and the thing about dying is a *lot* of words feel inadequate for my present situation.

Hey, do they waive student loans if the student has, you know, passed on? I never thought about that. You should ask, Parents! Play the dead kid card for all it's worth; I'm serious. That's what I would do.

As I was saying, it's nuts here. The first thing I see when I arrive (transcend? cross over? Man, I'm going to need to take a class on the proper terminology around here or something) is a group of six beautiful Dutch women presenting me with all of my favorite foods. Something about the Dutch, you know? Always the motherf*king Dutch. Like, every Dutch person I've ever met has been at *least* six feet tall, even the women, and they have the best accents. Less harsh than German, not as sing-songy as Swedish. Maybe my obsession has to do with those Dutch paintings we saw that one time at the Met. Remember, Mom? The way the light in all of them is softer somehow than real-life light, or at least New York light. I guess I associated heaven with that light as much as with the pearly gates and angels and whatnot.

Anyway.

So, these foods that the skyscraper-tall Dutch women have for me, they're my *specific* favorites: Domino's pizza with pepperoni and green peppers, filet mignon cooked with just the perfect amount of pink from Delfino's, and dragonfruit. Mountains of those pink mutants. I hadn't eaten dragonfruit since I was, I don't know, eight? Nine, maybe? I forgot that dragonfruit was even one of my favorite foods, like, if you had asked me at age 22 what my favorite food was, no way would that have crossed my mind, but then, BAM. Mountains of it with the motherf*king Dutch women, where I am deceased in motherf*king heaven, and I remembered the day that Grandma bought them for me like it was yesterday.

We were walking through Chinatown in August, and it was hot and smelled like fish, and I was pitching a fit because I just wanted to be home with my Gameboy and Pokemon, and she stopped and got me the weird alien fruit, and I was obsessed, man. I wouldn't shut up about that freaking fruit for a week, and then I moved on. The fruits felt a little like a message from Grandma, a reassuring, welcome-to-the-neighborhood type of thing. I hope I get to see her soon.

But back to the Dutch women (who have been in constant physical contact with me the entire time I'm eating my feast). While they're fawning over me, they ask me what my name is. I tell them, "Jake," but they giggle (of course they f*cking giggle), and say, "No, silly, you can have whatever name you want now!" Only it's in those perfect Dutch accents, so like, "No, sealee, ju caan haav watever naem ju waant nau!"

I pick Danger McSexface. I have been called Danger McSexface exclusively for three weeks. You must be so proud.

And get this: they also let you pick the *time of year*. It can be a season or one single day if you so choose. A buddy of mine, well, a guy whose beach bungalow is next to my castle, picked May 1st. He said that growing up his mom always made a big deal out of May Day, said it was a chance for regrowth and starting over. I guess that's what he needs here, so it's forever May 1st.

It's funny that the things parents said in life, which we brushed off while we were, you know, with you guys, are now what we glom onto. This guy – my neighbor – used to make fun of his mom for the May Day thing, and now it's literally his entire world.

For my time of year, I picked August. Not the muggy August city heat, I'm not crazy. I was specifically thinking of those summers as a kid when we used to go to Cape Cod just before school started. The ocean mist on my skin, the salty breeze as we all sat on the deck of that rental house, and Dad pouring water on our feet to get the sand off before we went inside. Even the sunburns. During the winters back home, with a scarf wrapped to my eyeballs and that god awful wind that cut through even the most "weatherproof" coats, I remember thinking I'd willingly be perpetually sunburnt if it meant I could have that ocean air. I had never felt anything like it, didn't think I ever would until here.

So, when I said "August," I was thinking of those Cape Cod Augusts, even though they were only for like three years when I was really little, and boom, they got it exactly right. Whoever's in charge here, if it is God or maybe an army of elves or Zeus, they really know how to do it. Like, without even having to explain what *kind* of August I meant, they knew exactly the one. It's like how Haagen Daas's mint chip is a million times better than Breyer's mint chip, and you don't exactly know how to explain why other than it just *is*. I bet if I were to go looking for mint chip ice cream in heaven (which is a thing I'm sure they have), it would only be Haagen Daas without me having to specify.

Up here in heaven - I keep saying "up" because that's always been my concept of this whole deal, but really I have no idea where I am geographically. We could be miles under the Atlantic or in the middle of a volcano on planet Xorantheon for all I know. I *feel* up, I suppose, or maybe that's just because it's been drilled into my brain from Sunday school and just about every book and every movie that ever dealt with the subject of heaven.

Everyone lives in whatever sort of house, skyscraper, compound, tipi, whatever you want. Sure, you get a lot of sprawling mansions, but there's also the people that want nothing more than to live in a pile of other people and fur blankets in the middle of the woods or what the hell ever so there they are. Me, I have a castle on the beach. Cozy, like you would have liked it, Mom. Full of fireplaces and paintings hanging on the exposed stone. It's a little dramatic, sure, but "castle" was the first housing structure that popped into my head when I got to choose, so here I am. I can change it whenever I want, but *why* would I downgrade from a castle? On the beach? You get my point.

Another interesting element of the hereafter - everyone in my little neighborhood, in my subsect of heaven, is under thirty. I imagine that might sound kind of depressing in theory, but it is really fun in practice. When you first get here, they have you exist with other people in your age bracket for six months as like orientation before you get to see everyone else. Dead relatives and whatnot. The people in charge here (still not sure what to call them since "angels" feels way off...they're more like those young hip college professors you'd want to get a beer with) say it's because it can be jarring to see someone you used to know right away, and they want you to get used to everything else first.

Some people don't ever leave their first part of heaven, from what I gather. But me, I'm stoked to meet up with some oldies. Or I wonder if I'll meet anyone famous. Eating those dragon-fruits with Heath Ledger or Kurt Cobain would be pretty sick.

It's funny too because technically it's not even really called "heaven" here. We can call it whatever we want. Which is nice in concept, but gets f*cking confusing. I've heard some people call it Sugar Frosty Wonderland, and some people call it Michigan.

For me it's Valhalla. Because that's a word for Viking heaven or something, right? Again, I'm not one for thinking too hard about these choices. I remember Grandma telling me about that, on a separate occasion from the dragonfruit. Speaking of, I'm excited to see her in a couple of months. I suppose I took that for granted, you know, that as soon as I died she'd be waiting for me with tea and lemon cookies and we'd hang out on her front porch, which would probably look exactly the same in heaven as it did on Earth. In life. Whatever. Gram was surprising, though, I bet wherever she lives now is nothing like her old house. An Italian-style villa, perhaps.

I mean, you guys think she's up here, right? As opposed to the alternative? Man, if you have some crazy shit on Grandma to tell me, now would be an excellent time, because I am really looking forward to those lemon cookies. I mean plus, if she's not here keeping tabs on me, there are a *lot* of other things I could get up to.

Well. So that's what's new with me. I live in my castle in Valhalla. I, Danger McSexface. And it's not so bad here. I mean, it's f*cking heaven. But sometimes I wonder. Like how you guys are doing, Mom and Dad. I imagine not so hot. Your recent college graduate son, who had the world in front of his happy-go-lucky nose, was shot and died instantly, no chance of saving him. I mean, shit, right? That's gotta be every parent's worst nightmare. No time to say goodbye, to see it coming or anything. Like, if I had to go and get myself killed, couldn't I at least have been in a coma first so that you could talk to me in my vegetative state? I'm not sure, would that have been better?

I guess that's not a fair thing to ask. I'm sure you're just trying to make peace with it all as it happened, and it's not fair of me to go poking around in that.

Part of me would like to think that as horrendous as this is for you, maybe I made it as easy for you as possible?

Ah, probably not. But hear me out, okay? At least you can go around knowing your son wasn't a *total* idiot who was shot just for being in the wrong place at the wrong time. He was shot when a bunch of asshole guys started harassing his friend Kristen, and it made his blood boil so hot and made red spots blur his vision, and so he needed to attack those monsters for yelling those disgusting things at her. For being so unbelievably *rude* and aggressive when she was just trying to take a shortcut home with her friend so they could enjoy more of the afternoon sunshine together.

Mom, you should have heard the things they were saying. I can't even repeat them, they were so vile, and Kristen, you both know her, she's a freaking angel who should never have to hear that kind of filth directed at her. She did nothing to deserve it, and I could tell she was getting so scared, because how could she not, and sometimes awful things happen to good people, but I couldn't let them hurt her. I couldn't let them *physically* hurt her, at least, so I decked the guy with the sideburns who seemed to be leading the pack, and then whoosh. That was it. You know, it wasn't even cold or painful, or anything like the movies depict, it was just *whoosh*. Lights out. Woke up in Heaven. Valhalla.

You know, yeah, she maybe would have been fine had I not done anything. Those whistles and words from those guys could have just been empty, pathetic jerkoff teasing, and then your son would have been shot for nothing.

But they could have been real. Real threats that turned into real actions that would have f*cked Kristen up for good. Not that my getting shot and killed in front of her is any sort of consolation prize. I'm not sure what happened after I was killed, which is kind of funny, but that's another thing the Cool Professors say: that they *highly* recommend not watching the moments immediately following your death. I can't help but wonder if those assholes got so freaked that they ran, and left Kristen there to deal with me on her own... Maybe the Cool Professors are right. Having to live with that image might actually be worse than being dead.

So, my point is, please don't hold this against her. It's not her fault, but my fault for having this hero complex or for just hating the idea of those jackasses getting away with being pieces of shit at my best friend's expense. And I wonder if my death had an impact on them? Who knows, but we can only hope, right? You know, if only one or two of the five of them was shaken up enough from having another person's death on their hands to never speak to a girl like that again, to never threaten or *do* anything to a girl like that, then just maybe isn't it worth it?

I guess it still might not seem like it to you. My sense of perspective is becoming very widely expanded up here. Like wars and things that seem like they last forever, with all of their death and destruction, don't last very long at all. They're over in like a millisecond in the real scheme of forever, and then the people who died come here for real forever, and it makes all of the suffering feel very, very far away. I'm still not sure how I feel about that yet, that as a reward for life we sort of get to distance ourselves from the bad stuff that's still very real and happening. No Facebook or Twitter feeds to keep us up at night in heaven. I guess I'll have a lot of time to philosophize about all that.

But okay, when you see Kristen or Mr. and Mrs. Davenport around, at the grocery store or the gym or some alumni functions or something (ugh, would you even go to those anymore?), I don't know, wherever you might see them around, just please don't hate them. Because it's not their fault that some people are assholes, and that some of those asshole people decided to prey on their magnificent daughter one afternoon and that your hotheaded son was there to try to protect her for whatever it was worth. So, if you could be nice, it would mean a lot.

I know this probably doesn't help, but I think I was in love with her. Kristen. I mean, I know I was in love with her. I've had a little bit of time to reflect up here, and I've realized that I was definitely in love with her. You probably could tell. She came over for Thanksgiving, after all, Mom, and no offense, but she ate your yam pie and pretended to *like* it. So, not to be even more depressing, but it seems like she would have been a keeper. Like, maybe instead of shouting at those guys I should have just grabbed her arm, whisked her away and told her that I had actually been madly in love with her since freshman year, and this whole best friend thing was great but I really, really f*cking hoped she felt the same because that would have been *spectacular.*

Hey, next time you have a kid, tell him not to be a wuss about things like that, okay? Tell him to suck it up and tell the girl that kind of romantic bullshit before he can't anymore.

Ah, shit. You're probably too old to have more kids, and if you're not, then this whole ordeal has probably shut you off from the idea, huh? I'm sorry about that, guys. Ruining your one go at it. You didn't deserve this.

I know this is shitty beyond belief, but I also know you're going to be okay because you're you guys, and you're the strongest people on the planet. So please don't pull some shit and get divorced over this, okay? May Day guy's parents - actually, now that I think of it, all of the other kids I've met up here who've died young have said that their parents got divorced over it- and you guys, I'm telling you, please don't. It's not worth it. You're way too... *you guys* for that nonsense. I mean, you're Kath and Pete, who met at Notre Dame! Who bonded over your love of international soccer, who dated from junior year on and got married in the spring of '94! For better or for worse! Til death do us part!

Not... Alright, but that was talking about *your* deaths, not mine.

I'm able to check in on you from here every so often. Once a week is what they say is "healthy," but they let you look in on the world whenever you want. I haven't been able to bring myself to see you guys yet, or Kristen, so I haven't, but I'm thinking about you all the time. And sometimes I have this...feeling, I don't know, it's hard to explain, that you're not doing great, like, as a unit. So, if you can snap out of that and make your marriage work despite your idiot son getting himself killed, that would be stellar. I'm rooting for you guys! Just like you were rooting for the US in the 2002 World Cup when we actually made it to the quarterfinals!

And I guess that's all there is to say about that.

So. This letter. You get one here, one letter to the living, like one phone call from prison. So, this is mine, and I know you won't get like, a physical letter because that's not the way it works, but I figured I'd pack it as full of detail as I can. The way it works is that once you send the letter the people you send it to *feel* it in these little ways. Like maybe you'll smell my Acqua Di Gio cologne, Mom (the one you thought was way too expensive and abrasive, and why did I need fancy cologne anyway?), on the street somewhere, and it'll be one of those things that makes you super nostalgic, and you'll breathe in the scent as deeply as possible even though you didn't care for it when I was alive. And then a week later, Dad, you'll hear my favorite song playing, "Don't Fear the Reaper," which you always made fun of me for liking so much. ("Blue Oyster Cult? Really, son?") I honestly didn't think about how ironic that title was until just now. I hope when you hear it play on whatever radio station is still playing Blue Oyster Cult, you appreciate the absurdity of it just a little bit.

So somehow these little signs and moments are supposed to convey everything I'm saying, which is a little frustrating because how can it? But I'm still telling you everything I need to tell you in the hopes that somehow, you'll just know. Like maybe the more details, the more whiffs of cologne or whatever.

And honestly, guys, don't worry about me. I'm chill here! Sure, there are some rather large hopes and dreams that I'll never accomplish, but the way I see it, all I can do is make room for other dreams here, right? Like dreams of Dutch women feeding me fruit.

I'm kidding. Kind of. I've actually been thinking of taking up cello again. As I've said, you can basically do whatever you want up here, and they *totally* encourage re-finding your lost passions, blah blah blah. But I figured that would make you happy, Mom. To know that I'm playing again.

Hopefully, when this letter is sent off, you'll catch a breeze of Cape Cod August air through your curtains. Better yet, I hope it happens when your windows are *closed,* to make an impact. The freakier, the better.

I love you.

Cheers from Valhalla,
Danger McSexface

IN THE COOL

Jennifer Bowen

The decision to throw out the festive fall wreath had been a last minute one. When Stevens' girlfriend - ex-girlfriend - Jenny, gave him twenty minutes to collect his things and get out of the apartment, he scoured for anything of his stashed under her bed. He saw the dried wreath next to plastic boxes of winter clothes. Jenny hated that wreathe. She wasn't someone to bring out seasonal decor for holidays. Stevens had bought it in error for her. He liked the burnt orange felt bow on top best. In an effort to appear thoughtful, he took the wreath with him to discard. Not that Jenny would look under her bed and notice, but you never know.

There was a strange rush to the relationship ending. Stevens eyed the silver mezuzah on Jenny's East Village doorframe (from another tenant) and counted the steps down to the ground floor (18), and when he slipped his key into her broken mailbox slot, he touched her name under the plastic cover (Jenny Suh). He dumped the wreath a few doors down because he didn't want her to see it or be overly obvious in his gesture. Somehow getting coffee at his usual café near 10th Street seemed too self-indulgent. So, he chose deli coffee on the corner of 6th and Avenue A. He ordered it black and as he stood outside near the wall of flowers for sale, he kept re-reading the iconic New York City Greek lettering on his paper cup: *We are happy to serve you.* He finished but wasn't ready to head to the subway. The late August heat caused sweat to pool around his neck and drip down his breastbone, so after a few minutes he pushed on towards the F train. As he passed by the building where he'd discarded the wreath, he saw someone had fished it out and tied the orange bow to a rusty peg that stuck out above the row of bins. Looking at the wreath hanging against the brick, his mind registered: *This means something.* But what it meant, he wasn't sure. Mostly he was glad he was getting out of the city for a while to stay at his sister's place upstate. Fall was just around the corner, but with the late August heat as tortuous as ever, it didn't seem like it. He was glad it was summer still. In truth, it might not turn cold for another month.

Sometimes when Stevens woke up still drunk it was like a silent hand clutched his shirt and physically lifted him up. That's what happened the next morning. He catapulted up when some higher entity, malevolent or benign he never knew, demanded he open his eyes. Fully clothed, he had made it upstairs to his sister's guest bedroom the night before. The lack of light was initially dizzying. Gathering his bearings, he tried to remember how he had gotten there. Then it filtered in. Face down on the couch; he awoke, a sheet over him. Parched, he'd made it to the kitchen. He'd rinsed his mouth with cool water and spat into the deep kitchen sink, wanting to rid himself of the sour berry taste at the back of his throat. The sheet still around his shoulders, cape-like, he'd forged his way back upstairs past his sister's closed door.

Stevens pushed himself up and into the hallway. He padded the few steps to his niece's room, its door halfway open. He hadn't seen her come home the night before, so he leaned in to make sure she had. She was curled up in the fetal position; her knees pulled tightly to her chest. Stevens frowned because it didn't look comfortable. Her white tank top and thin gray sweat shorts clung to her barely-there frame. She was leaving for college in a few days, and it reminded him of Jenny's frustrated demand: *Do anything with your life, Stevens! Anything! Get a dumb job, take up a hobby, go back to school for God's sake! So, you were successful once, well, time to rethink.* He stepped back sharply when his niece rustled and headed back to the guest room. Scrolling through saved tabs on his phone, he looked for nearby community colleges. Even though he was thirty, he was glad people often thought he looked younger.

And hobbies, Jenny? He had a fucking hobby, he thought. He ran. He stripped off his clothes, rummaged through his large black duffle bag that he had been living out for the last two weeks since Jenny dumped him (he told his sister he needed to stay two days, but who was counting) and changed into his sweat shorts and t-shirt. Propping his lean runner legs up against the bed, he did a few stretches. At the bottom of the duffle bag was a large bag of unsalted almonds. He grabbed a hearty handful and followed them with a good swig of water. Bouncing on the balls of his feet, he felt his tendons stretch and retract happily.

A minute later he was outside, feet hitting the pavement. The house was behind him. With every step, he sloughed off a layer of drunkenness. The humidity had broken. The air was a touch cool. The lush trees stood tall, everything budding and wet and ready. One thing in his life that still felt dependable was his body. Despite the cigarettes and the booze and the nights not sleeping much, he was addicted to running, and his efforts made him lean and toned in all the right ways. When he went in for his physicals, he concealed his recreational drug use (and daily glasses of wine at dinner and chronic love of chain-smoking into the night). Because of the omissions, he was always told he was doing great. Stevens wondered if his doctors knew that he fibbed a little and if maybe they admired him for it.

He would run to town and back. His watch read 7 AM, but it might as well have been 5 AM. No one was up. There was a sacredness to the morning like the quiet after he made love to Jenny when they both didn't speak for a few seconds. Some importance you couldn't quite define, but just felt. A feeling of: *I am at one with someone, there might be a God out there, and perhaps there is more light than darkness in the world after all.* Sweat spread across his brow. The running was so easy, glorious. Just his body jetting through space and time.

Then he saw them. Up ahead two pastel dots were walking in unison on the tree-lined, two-lane road. At first, he wasn't sure what he was seeing. Then he knew. Two Bruderhofs were out for a meditative walk (Patrons of a commune? Cult? New religion?). They were experiencing God just as Stevens was. A fresh, pine scent filled his nostrils as he ran faster. He couldn't wait until he could see them more clearly. When they did come into focus, he slowed his pace. Like he knew a miracle was about to flash in front of him, and he wanted to savor every moment.

The women were identical in height. He wondered if they were sisters. Partly it was their long light brown hair, stick straight, that swung behind their backs. They each wore lived-in Keds and long denim skirts that hit just above their ankles. They covered their heads in a pale lavender and off-white scarf respectively, showcasing their bird like features. High cheekbones, thin noses, and deeply set eyes. Not beautiful but not off-putting either. They looked like the kind of women where if you got to know them and unearthed their secrets and longings, you would love them. You'd savor hearing their deep guttural laughs when caught off guard. Then to say they were the most beautiful women in the world wouldn't be a fabrication.

Jenny was like that. A face in the crowd, pretty, but not a head-smacker. That was until you spoke to her, knew her, understood how she viewed the world and transversed through it.

Then she was a woman to whom you would consider complete and utter surrender.

Perhaps it was their shared view that life was a lot of mishaps and that one spent most of their time trying to scratch themselves out of a hole.

Not that they spoke about it directly on their first encounter at the Pyramid Club in the East Village. Both felt somewhat forced to be there (their respective friends brought them that night). They both drank the shitty gin and tonics and listened to the eighties cover band. When she bumped into him, she spilled his drink all over his sleeve. She used the bottom of her shirt to wipe up the mess. When she did, he saw a hint of her smooth, flat stomach. A mirror ball swirled on the ceiling not too far from them, so her face went in and out of shadows as they bantered.

Their jokes were dark in tone, and soon they were both laughing. He saw in her black eyes that she'd seen a thing or two, and no one had to spend long with Stevens to know the bloom had fallen off years ago. That first night they talked about why the phrase *Everything happens for a reason* was so fucked. They shared the times where they traveled solo (Lisbon, Paris for her; Tokyo, Morocco for him), and felt part of something bigger. And they discussed how when after spending all day alone they both wondered if loneliness was all there was. Just tea and bad TV and bed and nothing else? Never had he met someone who stepped so easily into the space right in front of him. He tried to persuade her to go home with him, but she just looped her fingers in between his pants and skin and said, *Maybe later.* It was enough to cause a schism in his psyche.

When they first slept together a month later, she tried to define the Korean experience of *Han* to him. It was as real a social construct as the American Dream she said. She explained how just about everyone had invaded Korea: the Chinese, Mongolians,

Japanese, Soviets, Americans. And Korea hadn't been able to do a damn thing about it. It bred a feeling of grief, of injustice going back centuries, of a deep desire to fight through the grief while acknowledging its eternal presence. As he watched her speak softly in profile against the fading Sunday afternoon sun, his worn Jersey cotton bedsheet barely covering her breasts, he knew this was a woman he could love.

The run had started to affect him. His limbs felt the first sign of strain. The joy of almost being pushed too far. When he passed them, they linked arms, and it reminded him of two sides of a heart necklace clicking together to become one. The Bruderhofs glanced at him once, and that was all. Just enough to say, *We see you, and we'll scream if you come closer.*

As his distance from them grew, he felt the final clutches of the booze slip away. He was now fully awake. Dull no more. He was running to town. Then he was going to turn around, go back to his sister's house, and get on the computer to look at the community colleges more in earnest. He'd lived under the glittering accomplishment of being a one-hit wonder, slightly famous, for too long. *Time to rethink,* Jenny said. Lastly, he'd call Jenny and tell her all he was feeling (alive, tingly, not willing to let real love go). He would fight this out with her. He wouldn't let his personal brand of Han lick him.

Stevens tried to find classes that appealed to him at Columbia Greene Community College, but the course names sounded vague, unpromising. After doing the family thing all day with his sister and niece, they had both gone out. He was alone in his car, and his finger hovered over his phone. He gave in and pressed play. The sound of his massive radio hit *That Night* filled the car. Stevens had heard the song so many times over the last ten years he had a hard time hearing the notes and melody. It was more of a blend of sounds.

The likelihood of Stevens running into someone he knew at one of the Saugerties bars was high, so he decided to head north. He called Jenny a second time but got her voicemail again. He ended the call without hearing the entirety of her recorded message and in an angry burst, threw his phone behind him into the backseat.

He knew the backroads along the Hudson River well. As a teenager he drove them furiously, taking each turn hard, tires skidding. Sometimes he'd end up in one of the sleepier towns and drive slowly up and down the streets. He enjoyed spying private moments: someone taking out a heavy bag of trash, two friends hugging goodbye in a doorway, siblings fighting over a toy on the front lawn. But then it was back to the main drag, going 80 miles an hour, destination TBD.

After speeding for a while, he made the turn off for Hudson. Now his pace was methodical down the main drag of Warren Street. He looked over the numerous furniture stores that had two arty names married by an ampersand, gorgeous late 19th Century Federal style buildings with large, black-shuttered windows. Some buildings had Widow's Walks (a railed rooftop where women would pace looking for their sailor men to come home); there were packed restaurants with more people standing outside (he almost slapped his cheek - *standing in line??*). The small bodega near the end of the drag was common in New York City but stood out here.

After he parked, he watched the comings and goings of locals in and out of the bodega with chips and sodas and light bulbs in hand who had been there before the gentrification really seeped in. Just being out of Saugerties, and in the relative bustle of Hudson normalized his heartbeat and kept the malaise that had crept in at bay. Beside his car was a piece of Americana art-work: an homage to the whaling history of the town. Two white whales enshrined in marble, patchworked with drawn images of old-timey Hudson. Stevens got out of the car and ran his hand over the bumpy surface. He wasn't totally sure what he want-ed out of the evening. The artwork reminded him that history was long behind him, but that the next five minutes were still undecided.

Walking the few blocks to his favorite watering hole The Half Moon Bar, he vowed not to drink. A seltzer and cranberry sounded quite refreshing. Hopefully, a local angsty band was playing, and he could fall away into the Friday night crowd. The Half Moon Bar had a throwback feel with a picture of a full-sailed shipping vessel between the *Half* and the *Moon* on its burgundy lettered sign. Even the diamond windowed doors and simple beige brick façade always made Stevens feel like he was stepping back in time.

As he crossed its threshold, he felt a luxurious assault on his senses. He adored bars. He loved the musty alcohol laden scents, the patchy lighting illuminating little moments (men cruising, women cruising, a casual makeout between strangers, the lone wolfs looking for prey, always someone too drunk and too loud, and at least one bartender as comfortable as fuck, the cock of the walk, slinging drinks with an expressionless gaze). A band was on in the back. The sign scotch-taped to the wall read: *Music Tonight - Pillars and Tongues*. Their tone was moody and almost ritualistic. It overwhelmed the bar in the best way possible. When music was that pervasive, it took away speech, leaving room only for roaming eyes. The lead singer moaned into the mike, swinging his long stick straight hair. The violinist and guitarist, both dressed in black, played trancelike behind him. A sprite of a girl with white blonde hair dressed in a pink plastic dress, no shoes, played an achingly beautiful riff on the accordion. The bar was packed, and instantly Stevens knew he came to the right place. He didn't recognize anyone.

He squeezed through the crowd and ponied up to the bar, finding an empty bar stool. The bartender, a woman in her early twenties with a black flop of hair, shaved sides, and a ring in her nose, lazily pushed a coaster towards him. "How can I help you?" she asked in a gravelly voice.

"Seltzer and cran. Lime please."

She wet her lips. Stevens spied the glint of a silver bolt in her tongue. Her dead gaze was now not so dead. She looked at him a beat longer. Stevens looked down. This was often how it started.

"Do I know you?" she asked.

He shook his head, not meeting her gaze. "I don't think so."

Sashaying back to get something from the other end of the bar, she kept her gaze on him as she scooped ice into a glass tumbler. The last thing he wanted was to talk to someone about his music. Often, he made up an identity and a career, and that worked just fine. *Biologist, Trend Forecaster, Fine Suit Maker.* Most people when they were drunk didn't ask too many questions, so the lies went over smoothly. To avoid her attention, he leaned back and watched two beefy biker dudes play a competitive round of pool.

A slim white arm draped over his shoulders. Startled, he turned to find a stranger standing inches from his face. She smiled a caught smile. She kept her light brown hair bobbed, her face makeup-free except for some smokey grey eyeliner. Her short black leather skirt with white snakeskin boots and shredded white t-shirt that read *If Only* made him sigh.

"Excuse me," Stevens said calmly. "You must have me confused with someone else."

She only gripped harder, pressing herself closer to him. He could smell her grape gum. "We don't know each other. I know *that*," she said.

Stevens' annoyance shifted, and he couldn't help but raise his eyebrows. Her eyes were clear, and he didn't think she was wasted. Wary still, mostly because she looked very young.

"You are the hottest guy here by a country mile, and I mean a *long* country mile."

The bartender slapped down his drink and threw a surly look their way. She threw most of the snark towards the young woman hanging off of him.

"What are you drinking?" she asked, smacking her gum.

"Hard stuff."

She leaned over and took a sniff. When she did, Stevens could see a hint of her lacy teal bra through her t-shirt. She took a second whiff, clearly knowing what she was doing, knowing she was being watched. Her elfish grin was infectious. Stevens didn't want to smile back at this banshee of a girl but couldn't help it.

She clapped her small hands together. "Knew I could make you happy."

"Did you?"

"Are you an alcoholic? Is that why you're not drinking?"

Stunned, Stevens double blinked. Her fearlessness was unnerving. "That's not a nice thing to ask someone."

Pulling back, she now leaned against the bar. "Oh? You want me to be nice?"

Stevens had been in this exact position many times. The easy, flirty banter, their hand on his knee shortly after, him leaning in to speak to them, lips inches from their ear, sometimes they recognized him, and it was all effortless. Sometimes they didn't recognize him, and he would keep it a secret until they were about to part ways. Once told, their arms would link with his, and they'd ask, *Where to next?*

Tonight, he wasn't in the mood to talk about what he had done in the past. His mind still fixated on doing something different for once *(school, yes!)* since he believed it would lead him back to Jenny. The thought of Jenny, her dark, luscious hair, an almost bossy way of speaking, and clearly-smarter-than-him kind of approach to big picturing almost every situation, should have dulled his blooming lust towards this slight girl in front of him. Illogically though, as if the two were connected, the girl's desire for him sparked his longing towards Jenny and then re-routed that longing back to the girl with the teal bra. Her hand was now on his knee.

"When are you buying me a drink?" she asked.

A small dose of reality hit. "Wait. How old are you?"

"Twenty-one."

"Sure. Let me see your ID."

She rolled her eyes and faked a pout. Then a look of suspicion came over her, "Wait, are you a cop?"

This made him laugh out loud and throw back his head. Then he looked her deep in the eyes. "Do I look like a cop?"

"No."

"I'm not. I promise. But let me see it anyway. Know what I'm dealing with here."

She fished around in her LP-shaped purse. Flipping open a ratty pale pink wallet, she handed him her ID. "Maybe this is weird foreplay for you?"

Shaking his head, he snatched it from her. He got her name. *Amy Perkins.* And then her age. "Nineteen, huh? Are you in college?"

"Parsons. In the city."

He reached for the lime on the rim on his glass and instead of squeezing it into his drink, took a long suck. Amy laughed at this and took her wallet back. Then she picked up his drink and took a large sip. When done, she wiped her mouth slowly with the back of her hand.

A small voice in his head said: *Go home, Stevens. Right now.*

He thought about what it was like to sleep with the same person for a year and a half, as he had with Jenny, a feat he had never accomplished before. There wasn't much room between Stevens and the next bar stool. Amy shimmied in place to the music. Pillars and Tongues had picked up the pace. The lead singer was now jumping to and fro on the makeshift stage. The whole crowd undulated. By the pool table, one of the bikers hit the last shot and shouted in victorious delight. Stevens saw the loser stalk about, trying to bend the pool stick in his hand. The bartender approached, one hand on her hip, and didn't say anything.

"Just my check," Stevens answered.

"It's on the house, fucker. You got soda water." Then she turned and walked to the other end.

Amy sported an exaggerated frown. "She's mad. I got to you first. I saw her eyeing you. Knew I had to work fast."

Jenny was probably at a lecture or taking in some obscure film at BAM. She was always bettering herself. Stevens lay down a twenty-dollar bill. Jenny could be with anyone. Some Deutsche Bank douche or the most obscurely famous painter in the world. She had that eerie quality of self-assurance that drew the masses to her. Or she was at some Italian restaurant in Chelsea, practicing her latest learned vocabulary with the waiter, making her date jealous as she twirled her *r*'s. Stevens slapped his face a few times. He felt like punching a wall.

Time to go, he told himself.

"Hey! Where you going?" Chirpy Amy looked authentically pissed that he didn't say goodbye as he got up off the stool.

Stevens saluted her. "I'm too old for you. Have a good night." As he walked towards the exit, he could feel her behind him. When he got outside, he turned and saw he was right.

Both her hands were up in the air, "What gives?"

"What do you mean?"

"You're leaving?"

"Yeah." Stevens started up the inclined street to his car. The train tracks were to his left. They were always a weird pull for him. Some part of him wanted to lay down in the center and like a magic act, see if the train would pass right over him. All the light had escaped from the sky in the last twenty minutes. Stevens could feel the Hudson River on his skin.

Amy side skipped next to him, undeterred. "Thing is, I know you like me."

"Yeah?"

"I could feel it in the bar."

She had the smile of a child in trouble. All bright eyes and secrets. Then she tripped, her side skipping coming to a stop due to uneven cement. Stevens reached out, caught her by the elbow. Her light green eyes sparkled with devilish delight. "So, you're that guy."

"What?"

"Savior type."

Once she was fully upright, Stevens let go and stuffed his hands into his tight jean pockets. His throat was burning for some whiskey. Only two more blocks to his car. He had to shake her. "I have a girlfriend."

"No, you don't."

"How do you know?"

"Because online it says Stevens Miller and his girlfriend Jenny Suh just broke up."

This stopped him cold. A prickly feeling sprung up behind his neck. How had he missed this? "I thought you didn't know me."

"I lied. I'm sorry." She shrugged, not looking sorry at all.

What did it matter? People hit on him all the time. They were hungry to touch a bit of fame even if his was faded. He resumed his pace up the hill. He felt like running. They walked in silence back to his car. Stevens stood by the driver side, not sure whether to unlock the door. Amy's silence had shifted into a sullen look. Her eyes were as wide as they could be, and a worry squiggle had sprung up between them.

As Stevens lingered, she approached him and said in a soft, sweet voice. "Am I not pretty enough for you?"

Stevens set his car keys on the hood and took a step closer. "No, not at all. You're beautiful."

"So, what gives?"

"I just turned 30; you're...19? What do you want to do with me?"

Amy turned and walked towards the Americana whale artwork he had spied earlier. With her pointer finger, she followed the outline of each whale and hummed softly. Her sudden retreat was baffling. Stevens casually walked up beside her.

"Hudson was a whaling and shipping town. Did you know that?" he said.

She smiled a little. "Is that why I see whale this and whale that everywhere?"

"Yup. On the signs and address numbers on houses."

A car drove by with a bunch of young kids in it. The music blared. They both looked. For a brief second, they could hear the kids' voices and laughter falling out of the car. Then they were gone, and it was silent again. Stevens suddenly felt an ache like being in his own body was too much of a burden. Amy turned and brushed his dark hair out of his eyes. Her fingers felt impossibly smooth on this skin.

"What was it like to have such a hit record?"

"Crazy."

"I remember the video for *That Night* playing on MTV. My older sister had your *Rolling Stone* cover framed in her room. You didn't want to put out any records after that?"

Clearing his throat, Stevens said, "I did. One. It bombed."

Amy shrugged again and shivered, saying nothing. Her pale arms dangled by her side.

"Do you need a ride home or something?"

"I have girlfriends back at the bar. Can we sit for a minute in your car? I feel a little dizzy."

"Sure." Stevens walked back to the car and unlocked it. But instead of getting into the passenger side seat, Amy got into the back. Stevens' mind raced for a second, and then he joined her. He sat there, hands clasped.

"How did you write that first album?"

Stevens remembered being nineteen himself the night that started it all. His sister, ten years older, was his guardian for so long he mostly knew their parents from pictures and stories. He rarely saw his sister as a sibling. She was something closer to his second half – he wasn't quite whole without her around. That night they were drinking. After a few glasses, red wine stained their teeth. Hers were a berry tint, his a rich blood color. Instead of doing the right thing and calling it a night, he fell face forward into some incongruous need to be loved. Baffled, she pushed him off of her, and for the next half hour, they just sat in the living room, saying nothing. The next morning, he ran off to New York City and poured that night into his music. When asked about the origin of the song, he could never disclose the truth. He thought one day he might shock the world with the grotesqueness of his ancient needs that confused even him. Instead, he gave his standard answer, "I can't say."

"Meaning?"

"It's a secret."

This always intrigued people and Amy was no different. It was also a version of the truth. She ran her hands along the back of one of the car seats. "Your car is kind of a junker. I love it."

"Thanks. I guess."

He watched her fingers dance across the headrest for a full minute. Then she lightly caressed his cheek with the same dancing fingers. Her skin was smooth. No lines. He loved that she wasn't wearing makeup except for the gray around her eyes which looked like a bullseye. He could see a few freckles on her nose and a pink patch of irritation on her left cheek. In New York City there were always lights and people and action. But on the far end of Warren Street, everything was dark and undisturbed. Stevens felt alone with Amy in the best way possible. He was thinking of kissing her when she kissed him.

Her warm mouth met his, and she kissed his top and bottom lip separately. Then she increased the pressure and opened her lips slightly. Stevens ran his fingers through her shaggy bobbed hair. Her breath still had a delightful taste of grape Kool-Aid. She pushed him back and straddled him, taking his face in her hands. He yanked up her tight black leather miniskirt, and she bumped her hips forward, so she was even closer to him.

Fucking Jenny. She was probably eating gnocchi and sipping Pinot Grigios on 9th Avenue with some man who would never love her the way Stevens did. If she couldn't grasp the seismic mistake of breaking up with him, well, it wasn't his job to explain it. She could nosedive into her Han. And he his.

Amy moaned and went for his buckle. She lifted his shirt and kissed his concave chest. He felt her small breasts under the teal bra. Each mound told him a profound truth: *There has always been this between two people. Let yourself go.*

He did.

He peeled off her shirt, then quickly undid her bra. She pulled down his pants. He flipped her onto her back. Kissing her over and over again, he lay on top of her, slowing everything down. He teased her until he slowly sped up. She clutched him, face tilted upward, her small neck so vulnerable, so exposed until he grunted for her to come. *Right now,* he demanded. And she did, wilting, falling inward, shuddering, and then he did too with slow, luxurious pulses, their bodies coming together.

After, he let his full weight fall onto her. They breathed in unison. She tickled the back of his neck, bringing him back to reality.

I'm naked in my car.

He pulled out and reached for his pants. She silently found her bra, shirt, underwear, and skirt. Within minutes they were fully clothed again with flushed faces.

A bit wooden, Amy asked, "Do you have a lot of one-night stands?"

"Do you?"

"No."

"Good."

Amy cocked her head. "Why, good?"

He leaned back, and his eyes sought the whale art just outside the window. Suddenly, all the closeness and longing he felt went away. What was Amy's last name? He knew five things about her, at most. Plus, she was nineteen. Scratching his cheek, he said, "I was just thinking of my niece. She's only seventeen, so a bit younger than you, and I hope she doesn't do this sort of thing."

Amy rummaged in her purse and found a new piece of gum. "How do you know she hasn't already?"

"Because she's not like that."

"Not like what?"

"She's sensitive and smart."

Amy needled his side with her finger. "She can be all those things and still want to get fucked."

A small amount of bile rose up in Stevens' throat. He pushed Amy's hand away. "You don't know anything about me or my family."

"Some things are universal."

Stevens looked at his phone to see if he had any missed calls or texts. Not one. "She's on a date tonight, my niece. Hope she's alright."

"She's fine."

"I'm not so sure."

Amy cocked her head. "Why are you so worried? Are you a creep or something?"

Stevens looked up. "What do you mean?"

Amy opened the car door. "There's something off about you. I don't know what it is, but it's there. I better get out of here before you make a skin suit out of me."

Stevens pulled at his loose t-shirt, suddenly heated. "What?"

Leaning back into the car, Amy gave a wonky smile and winked. "I'm just fucking with you."

"I hope so."

"I *am* being serious now. I have to ask you something." She leaned down further so he could peek inside her shirt again. A hint of teal taunted him. "You'll probably think I'm a skanky loser, but I am doing this media project about encounters with strangers. I won't use your name. I promise. But can I get your picture? Not your face. Just the back of you, right now, in the car. I'll probably write a little text along with it. I won't use your name. I swear on my life. It goes up the second week of September at Parsons."

Her voice had lost the childlike quality. There was something direct about its tone. Stevens didn't consider himself naïve. Still, he believed what she said. So, he turned around, and she clicked her phone a few times, then showed him the shots. His thin torso and scraggly dark hair in the backseat of his shitbag car. She winked again and brought her lips to his cheek. Then she fluttered her eyelashes in a butterfly kiss on his neck and whispered, *I hope another secret thing happens and you write a killer third record. Call me crazy, but I think it's in you.* Then she turned and headed back to the bar, face down into her phone.

He got out of the car and watched her leave. He pictured his 19-year-old self, a ghost now, a stranger. Pulling out his phone from his back pocket, he brought up the website for Columbia Greene Community College. Its logo was a vague looking yellow flame, pea green on one side, burnt orange on the other. A double coo sounded from an oncoming train heading north toward the location of the college. He made a note in his phone: *Young Amy's Show - 2nd week of September.* He didn't know if he'd be back in the city. Probably not, but still. The wind came in and rustled a few trees at the end of the block. The night sky looked blacker somehow. Stevens grabbed his worn-out blazer and flipped up the collar. Like that, the Fall cool had arrived without any warning.

October

LEGENDS

Michael Owl

I t's going to come down one way or another," the arborist
said. "You might as well control where it lands."
Never ask a barber if you need a haircut, Juan thought
as he checked in with Barbara.

"Conference?" he asked.

"No. Let's do it."

And with that, Juan realized he'd never need to buy firewood again, or at least for the foreseeable future. Unspoken was
the notion that the recent storm provided cover for the insur-
ance company to pay for the removal of the tree. A few thousand saved, a few thousand earned. Juan had two thoughts as
he signed the paperwork. I'm doing something smart, and I'm
doing something shady. Mixed within those two thoughts was
a vague sense of dread like he was stepping out into unknown
territory. He was not, by nature, a risk taker.

The tree was the last in a lineage of towering oaks that had
lined the drive up to the main house of a nine hundred acre
plantation. You could still picture it if you tried really hard
and had a copy of the old photo handy. Otherwise, it looked
like any standard suburban house in any well-to-do southern
neighborhood.

The morning the ancient oak came down, Juan stood at the
edge of the yard watching the removal team work. Like a dis-
passionate autopsy, they dismantled the aged giant in sections,

saving the stump for last. With a decadent smell and a ripping much louder than he anticipated, Juan saw the roots wrenched from the ground. He wondered how far under his yard they'd grown and if parts of them would remain long after the removal team left.

Juan hadn't been excited to move here. He would point out that while The Verandas only vaguely alluded to the area's ignoble past, it was, in fact, a plantation at some point, and not all that long ago in the scheme of things. There was no telling the suffering that occurred here, and is this really where they wanted to raise their child?

Barbara dismissed his concerns, reminding him that before the atrocity of slavery occurred here, probably thousands of Native Americans died of smallpox and other diseases from the European "settlers." And before that, she said, different tribes probably battled and killed each other, and way before that, there were countless animals roaming about. You know, she said, most animals in nature are eaten while they're still alive.

Her argument: if you're looking for a place to raise Juliet that doesn't have a horrible history of death and tragedy, I don't think you're going to find it. Look around. It's all a graveyard.

Juan didn't know what to say to that, so he said yes to moving. Besides, he found her dark side sexy.

She was the realist. Juan was the dreamer.

It was now officially latish, ten o'clock, and the fire was dying. Juan was thinking about reviving it. For ten minutes, he had been willing his body to get up and grab another log or two, but the Adirondack chairs they'd bought were hard to get out of, and oh so comfortable. The five beers he'd had and the tiniest of tokes from Joey's one-hitter weren't helping either. And he'd need to go around to the back of the house, where the new wood pile sat under a makeshift awning. It was ugly, but it worked for now. He'd buy a proper shed for it in a few weeks.

Juan looked at his wife Barbara and tried to read the tea leaves. Her head was down looking at the baby monitor app on the phone, sandy blonde hair obstructing her face.

Inconclusive. There hadn't been a trick-or-treater in fifteen minutes, and it looked like Joey's wife Michelle had stopped drinking her wine. It was probably time to wind things down.

Juan hated winding things down.

"Any action over there?" he asked. Barbara showed him the screen on the phone. Juliet slept peacefully in the grayness of the black and white camera, her tiny hands holding the swaddle up around her neck. Juan grabbed the phone and showed it to Joey and Michelle.

"Have you ever slept that good?"

"I might tonight," said Michelle. "I think it's time, honey."

Joey ignored her.

"Trick or treat!"

Two hooded figures had snuck up the slate walkway. Possibly Jedis, from the cloaks they were wearing.

"Looks like we're still in business," said Juan.

Joey did the honors this time, giving each of them an extremely large handful of mini-candy bars. Juan and Barbara had nearly fought earlier in the evening over whether to give out full-sized candy bars or not. Barbara won.

"How about one more round?" said Joey.

"Let's not," said Michelle. "It's late, and Juliet might resent me if went and crawled into her crib."

"You're welcome to stay," Juan said. He could feel a look coming up from where Barbara was sitting. Well too bad. He'd tried to read her. Maybe if she didn't have her head in the baby monitor all night, he'd have known what she was thinking.

"We haven't even told ghost stories, yet. Wasn't that the whole point?" said Joey.

It was true. Juan had always wanted to have a big Halloween storytelling party, one where they'd put out a thousand votive candles and shut off all the other lights. They would sit around and see who could tell the best story. For the second year in a row, they'd settled for having their neighbors over to drink wine around the fire pit, while they gave candy out to the trick-or-treaters.

"Tell you what. You grab a bottle of wine, and I'll get a log or two," Juan said to Joey.

"I'm going to be right here if you need me," Michelle said as she folded her tiny, gymnast body into the chair. "And I may be napping." Not for the first time, Juan thought she must have been a cat in a past life.

Juan squeezed Barb's shoulder as he went by wishing she was as laid back as Michelle. He knew he'd be hearing about this later. So be it. It was Halloween. The air was crisp. They had plenty of firewood and almost as much beer.

Juan gathered as much wood as possible, carrying a huge stack in his arms like a lover across the threshold of the honeymoon door or a soldier with a fallen mate. This was the first of the "new, old wood" as Juan thought of it that he'd used. October had been unseasonably warm until this week, and Joey'd brought some wood from Publix that they'd burned first. Juan felt something with many legs crawling slowly on the back of his neck but decided to ignore it and walk faster rather than drop the wood and scratch. When he arrived back at the fire, he was winded but pleased to see the wives' wine glasses were full and the rest of the bottle leaned against the cooler.

Juan added some wood to the fire and stoked it, then watched as the new, old wood brought the blaze to life. It made a ghostly whine as air escaped from the tiny holes deep within it. It smelled dank and ancient, and the flames quickly shot high into the air.

Juan looked around the yard watching the light make shadows. All of the mammoths had been felled. Juan imagined the former row of trees guarding the area, the canopy covering anyone traveling up the main road. Protecting. Standing witness. He had planted several azaleas where the last tree had been, but so far nothing had taken hold. He wondered if the land was insulted by the choice, preferring the ancient trees to the nursery-bought bushes. He was lost in these thoughts when he felt a clap on his back.

"I'm going to go first, okay?" Joey said.

"Sure," Juan muttered, reaching into the cooler to grab another beer. He wondered how high he really was to be thinking about the trees like that.

Joey cleared his throat and wiped his beer-soaked mustache with his sleeve. The red flannel shirt looked like a jester's costume in the shadow and light of the fire.

"Is this going to involve an Indian burial ground?" said Michelle, who was still awake despite all appearances.

"No, it will not."

"Oh good."

"I'm kidding. Of course, there's an Indian burial ground. This whole hemisphere is an Indian Burial Ground. Hell, we live off Indian Trail Road. It's not because of the great samosas."

Barbara laughed. Juan thought that was a good sign.

Joey took a long swig of beer as the wind blew hard, causing the fire and smoke to rush towards him.

"The gods are angry," said Juan, enjoying being upwind.

Joey inhaled, his shoulders lifting, but rather than speaking, he coughed, gagged, and rather violently shook, until he was able to rest his hands on his knees, bent over trying to catch a clean breath. After he recovered and stood up, he rubbed his eyes hard. They were red and irritated. Then he suffered one last convulsion, the kind where chills rush through the length of the body, the kind that made Barbara's grandmother say someone had walked over your grave.

"That's a good story. Maybe some words next time instead of just the coughing and interpretive dance," said Juan.

Joey's voice was detached. Metallic. Maybe he didn't get the joke. The next words came out hard. "I just remembered a new story. I'm going to tell it. From what I understand, this actually happened and took place really close to here.

"A few years ago, a student doing research on local legends found a newspaper article interviewing three women whose grandmothers had all experienced, what was described in the article as a supernatural event. This student went to talk to the women, all over the age of eighty, and this is what they told him:

"On Halloween, almost one hundred years ago, their grand-mothers' were each visited by a spirit. The spirit took the form of a woman who appeared to be in her twenties, dressed in a thin, white nightgown. They said it moaned, a horrible low pitched sound that they felt in their chest more than they heard in their ears. However they sensed it, all of them said they'd never heard a sound more mournful, and because of this, they called it the Ghost of Inconsolable Grief."

"Catchy," Barbara said.

Joey plowed through.

"The ghost, while moaning, also kept making a gesture with her arms." Joey held his arms in a circle like a cradle and looked down lovingly at his empty arms. He did this for a little longer than seemed reasonable, and Juan was about to say something when Joey's arms lurched out in front of him like he was grabbing something just out of reach.

"Over and over again, she did this." Joey completed the sequence again. "Always making that terrible sound."

Michelle made a moaning sound like an angry, wet ferret that quickly devolved into giggles.

"Thank you, dear," Joey said. "Very helpful." Michelle smiled up at him.

"Now, the women all agreed that this spirit somehow wanted them to help her, even though they didn't know with what. The moaning and the gesturing got louder and faster. The spirit's face went from begging to frustrated, and to angry, and finally to fury. The women sensed they were letting the spirit down, and it was becoming desperate, but they didn't know how to help.

"At that point, they said the ghost started going into different rooms of the house like she was searching for something. And this is where their accounts differ. For two of them, the spirit went methodically through every room of the house and then just left, making one last final moan that was more of a scream and then disappeared.

"For the third, the ghost also searched through every room of the house until it found what it was looking for. The nursery. And when the woman caught up to it, she said the ghost looked like it was trying to pick up her baby. She said it was trying to hold her sleeping baby.

"Of course the mom freaked out and marched over to the crib to hold her child. When she did, a part of her passed through the ghost. She said it felt like mist, like a cold fog during an early morning hike in the forest. When the mom picked up the baby, the ghost pointed at her and gave her the most piteous, tragic look she'd ever seen. Then it disappeared. The baby cried for two days straight after that."

Joey lowered is head and stared into the fire.

"Afterwards," he whispered, "even though it didn't make sense, all three women couldn't shake the feeling that they'd missed an opportunity to save this spirit, to help her, and by helping her, reduce the untold amounts of suffering in the world."

The silence lasted a few moments, broken only by the crackling of the fire. The new, old logs seemed to be doing their part to enhance the moment.

"Help her how?" asked Juan.

"In good time, sir." Joey paused for another swallow of beer. He was enjoying the attention when the wind kicked up again, this time infecting both him and Michelle. Michelle shuddered and tried to hide her eyes from the smoke.

"How come this wind never blows in your direction?" asked Joey.

"Because I sit on the other side," Juan said. "How did the ghost want them to help her?"

"By stopping her from hurting her child," said Michelle, unfurling her body and sitting up. Everyone looked at her.

"How'd you know that?" asked Joey. "I just heard this story, and I don't even remember where."

"I've heard it somewhere. Or something similar. Let me refill my glass, and I'll tell you," she said.

Barbara's eyes went back to the monitor. Juan took a couple of steps over and put his hand on her shoulder.

Earlier that evening, after the sun had just dipped below the horizon, Juan lit the candle on the jack-o-lantern. Then he came inside, turned up the volume on the speaker, and started singing along with the tune. Monster Mash was a favorite of Pandora's Halloween playlist, and since he knew Barbara hated it, he sang with extra gusto.

His efforts were not wasted.

Barbara came down the stairs carrying little Juliet and flashed Juan a look.

"Remember, it's not that long until Christmas, and you'd better believe that Grandma will be getting run over by a reindeer often and loudly." Her threat was made more ominous by the flirty smile that accompanied it.

"I got to live for today, baby, and do the Monster Mash. THE MONSTER MASH." He turned the volume up further as he said it.

Barbara went over to the couch and pulled two costumes out of a Party City bag. "Moment of truth. Angel or Demon?"

Juan took Juliet and held her high in the air. Juliet smiled her lopsided grin, and a little drool dropped down onto Juan's shirt. "Well given last night's stellar performance, I'd say Angel. What baby sleeps through the night like that? I guess that new NyQuil baby formula worked."

"Oh, you have the funniest Daddy don't you, Juliet. He thinks he's so funny. Are you ready?"

"I'm ready. Hey, Joey texted, and they have to hit another party before they're coming over – "

"This isn't a party. It's a drink on Halloween. It's low key, remember? What time are they coming?"

"A little after nine."

"I'm not keeping her up that late."

"That's fine."

"But they won't see how cute she looks in her costume."

"Given what happened, that's probably for the best."

"Are they trying again?"

"Yeah. At least the trying part is still fun."

"Until it isn't."

●   ●   ●   ●

"I think I know where it starts." Michelle was standing, her full glass of red in her left hand swaying dangerously as she rocked back and forth.

The other three were huddled close together on the other side of the fire. Joey had joined Barbara and Juan in the one quadrant that for some reason was smoke-free. Only Michelle received the occasional gust.

"Hundreds of years ago, for the two weeks leading up to All Saint's Day, strange things began to happen around here. A cow was found mutilated. A field of corn was destroyed. Fish were found floating dead in the stream. These things didn't happen all at once, but every few days something mysterious and damaging would occur. Since this was a rural area, word spread slowly. But eventually, most of the town agreed that something bad was happening, and it was getting worse.

"Everyone was charged with paying special attention to the strange. To notice. To study. And to report back the next Sunday, All Hallow's Eve.

"When next Sunday arrived, the villagers were frenzied. While there were some more reports of odd little things happening, what scared them most was their dreams. All of them, to a person, had nightmares. And all of these dreams involved a figure they named The One. In the dreams, The One demanded they worship Him. That they honor Him. That they sacrifice to Him. Even the minister, who looked like he hadn't slept at all that week, told the congregation that he too had been visited by The One. Oddly enough, none of the villagers could describe The One. But they knew what it wanted.

"The men argued over what should be done. They stood in a group in the middle of the town square, talking over each other. Pushing and shoving ensued. Then someone threw a punch. And just as it looked as if an all-out brawl was going to break out, an elderly man in a cloak came up to the group. He was crying.

"'She didn't mean it. It wasn't her. It was something in her.' The man kept repeating this as he worked his way up to the minister, his eyes focused on the bundle he carried, not noticing that everyone had gone silent and stared at him. He stumbled up to the minister and handed him the blankets. 'Please,' he said. 'Do something.'

"The minister unwrapped the blankets. There wasn't a mark on the baby. You could almost persuade yourself it was just sleeping. Almost.

"The man led the townsmen to his farm. They found his daughter in the front yard mumbling prayers to The One, and repeating to herself, 'It needed you, it needed you, it needed you.'"

Michelle let it settle for a bit, pleased with herself. She took a long drink from her wine glass nearly emptying it.

"You can guess the rest. They took her to the square and burned her."

An owl hooted, the fire cracked, and Barbara rose, her eyes on fire.

"Leave," she said and walked into the house.

Twenty minutes later Juan had picked up the empties outside and started the kettle inside. He'd had the tiny hope of sitting alone with a whiskey by the fire, so he let it continue to burn. It was dying down, anyway. On his phone, he saw Barbara's shadow over the still sleeping Juliet. He put the phone away wondering why he felt uneasy.

He handed Barbara a mug of chamomile as she came down the stairs. Her eyes seemed like they had calmed down the tiniest fraction, so he gambled.

"I'm trying to think of an equivalent, but all I can come up with is telling nothing but hurricane stories to a guy who just bought a beach house." It didn't get a laugh, but it didn't get his head bitten off either.

"I think she is seriously fucked up," Barbara said and sat down on the comfy reading chair.

Juan thought he had better keep his distance, so he sat on the couch. He pawed at a seam beginning to come loose.

"You don't agree?" she said. A challenge.

"Yeah. Batshit crazy. They're going through something, no doubt," he said. "I don't think we realize how lucky we are, to have taken the goalie away and gotten pregnant so fast." He sipped his tea, eyeing her. "I'm pretty damn talented. The seed is strong."

A half smile, and then a throw pillow in flight that barely missed his head.

"So that's why they're called that," he said.

Another smile. Three-quarters this time. God bless her, she didn't stay mad for long.

"What was your favorite costume? The sexy dentist or the sexy air traffic controller?" he asked. Barbara walked over and sat on the other end of the couch, her feet landing in his lap. Juan rubbed them.

"The sexy cartographer gets my vote," she said.

Juan trailed one fingernail down the middle of her foot. Just enough so she'd laugh but not pull it away.

"She's really out, isn't she?" Juan said.

"It's kinda nice."

"Yeah, it is."

"No guests next year, all right?"

Juan agreed. "Definitely."

"Come here."

He moved towards Barbara, and they kissed.

A small noise upstairs.

"Are we really that stupid to have jinxed it?" Barbara asked.

"Why yes. Yes, we are."

They waited, ears angled upstairs. Nothing.

"Looks like we got a reprieve." They kissed again.

"You smell like pot," she said.

"In a good way?" He kissed her one more time, but she pushed him away.

"Another cup of tea and I will ignore your hippie ways," said Barbara.

They'd had ups and downs in their six years of marriage, but things had settled down nicely as of late. Juan grabbed their cups and walked over to the kettle.

"So if our ridiculously rude friends hadn't told ghost stories clearly meant to offend us and make their shitty lives better, what story were you going to tell?" Barbara asked.

Still not out of the woods. "I don't know. All the scary stories I know end with, 'and the call was coming from inside the house,'" he said and gave a short maniacal laugh.

As he did, his phone buzzed, and they both jumped. A text. "Jesus that scared me. It's Joey, apologizing. Says they are both mortified. Not sure what came over them. Maybe had too much to drink. Very sorry. Etcetera, etcetera."

He held up the phone to her. "What do you want me to say?"

The phone buzzed again. "He says he doesn't even know where they heard those stories."

Juan handed her the phone and went back to pour the tea. Barbara studied the texts. "Let 'em stew for a minute. I'm putting some PJs on. Is the fire out?"

Juan looked out the window and silently said goodbye to his alone time. "Not yet."

"Will you handle that?"

"Yeah," he said and walked out the door leaving the tea to steep.

Juan watched the dying fire come to life briefly as the strong October wind kicked up again. The tiny embers reminded him of a dying animal rousing itself for one more attack. The smoke got in his eyes, so he rubbed them with one hand while using the other to shovel some dirt on the fire. The smell of the smoke reminded him of playing hide-and-go-seek in his basement as a child. They lived in a stone and wood house, and playing in the deep underground area was like visiting a strange land. A chill ran down his back.

When he came back in the house, Barbara was cupping her tea and wearing her footy pajamas he'd bought her for Valentine's one year.

Juan gathered the plates they'd laid out for snacks and began the process of rinsing them off and loading them in the dishwasher.

"You know, I do know one ghost story I could've told."

"Is it about a rude couple who can't conceive?" Barbara winced at her own comment. "I'm sorry. That was mean."

"No, not exactly," Juan said clearing his throat. "This one takes place thousands of years ago. At the time, this area was much more wooded, and the people who lived here saw nature as an extension of themselves. They believed in many spirits: the trees, the sky, the birds. All of their natural surroundings had a different spirit that governed them. But there was one spirit, The Creator, who ruled them all. It was the Creator who ensured the harvest would be bountiful; who saw that the hunting would yield enough meat; who made sure the river would not dry up or flood. The spirits and the people lived harmoniously with the Creator. Should the Creator decide that a sparrow's time was over, then, it was over. Same with the tribal Chief, the Medicine Women, or a Brave. If it was your time, then it was your time, and they all accepted it."

Juan continued to work at the sink. Barbara stiffened, looking at Juan's back and tightened her grip on her mug.

"But for three years in a row, the harvest was not bountiful. The animals dodged the hunter's arrows, and the river flooded in the wet season and turned to dust in the dry. Many died. Many more became sick. The people despaired.

"But at the new year ceremony, one of the elders thought there might be a way to prevent these tragedies. Surely the Creator needed their deaths from time to time. Otherwise, why would he make these things happen? Why didn't they live forever? There had always been death. But maybe instead of needing so many people to die, there was a way to give the Creator a special death. A death so meaningful that the Creator would accept it as a stand-in for all the other deaths he was due that year."

"If this any way involves killing a baby, we're getting a divorce. I mean it. Tomorrow. Divorce." She tried and failed to make it sound like a joke.

Juan shut off the sink and closed the dishwasher. He slowly turned around, his eyes reddening as he spoke and walked towards her.

"Oh, it didn't have to be a baby. The age of the sacrifice wasn't important. What was important is that it was the Chief's child. It could be a full grown man if that were the case."

Juan's eyes gleamed, and Barbara put her body between Juan and the staircase that led to Juliet's room.

"Juan?"

He continued towards her.

"If the Chief had more than one child, the children would pull dried beans from a pouch, one of which had been made dark from a fire. The scorched bean meant you'd won. You were the sacrifice."

He was almost to her now.

"When the practice first started, some of the chiefs rebelled. But the Medicine Man outranked the chiefs in matters of the spirits. And then the people accepted it, Barbara, because there really is a Creator who does indeed demand sacrifice. Did people really think that all the deer meat and skins and corn, and all the furniture and the dishwasher and the cars were free? That there wasn't some sort of price demanded for all of this bounty? I mean, look around! Look at this house!"

They were eye to eye at the foot of the stairs.

"You're scaring me," Barbara whispered.

"Don't be scared. It's going to be okay," the thing in Juan said.

They were both still for a moment, then Barbara raced up the stairs and skidded left into the nursery before Juan could make it inside the room. She locked the door just before he tried to turn the knob.

He slammed into it, but it held.

Barbara reached for her cell phone in her pocket, but her pajamas had no pockets.

Juan sang. The melody was almost like an Irish bar song, one where men would sing and sway, arms around their shoulders, but the words Juan sang were from another language.

The door pounded again. This time the hinges began to give.

"You've got to stop, Juan. You're scaring me. You're scaring Juliet. Do you understand? You are scaring your daughter!"

Another pound.

"Stop it. Right now, Juan. Stop it."

Barbara ran to the window, opened it, and looked down at the front yard and the street beyond it. She looked for late night trick-or-treaters or teenagers vandalizing the sidewalk, anybody. But the street was empty. She yelled out anyway, but there was no response.

The window let out onto a sloping roof. She placed a leg out the window and decided there was zero chance she wouldn't fall. With her luck, she'd fall into the fire, which still had small, red lines of embers pulsing through it like veins feeding a heart. A thin trail of smoke wafted through the window, and a slight chill ran down her spine as she smelled the wood char, reminiscent of roasted marshmallows and the danger of being young and close to a fire.

Crashing noise against the door again. Different this time, in a single spot, and repeated rapid fire. She could hear the door beginning to crack, and then at once, it splintered, and two prongs of a hammer jutted through.

"Stop it, Juan. I need to tell you something."

Juan continued to hammer the door. She saw his fingers emerge from the hole desperately reaching for the knob, his fingers just glancing off it. She went to the window again.

Juliet's cries were getting louder now. Barbara picked her up and took her over to the window. She took a deep breath and tried to yell one last time as loud as she could, but only coughing and wheezing came out.

She rubbed her eyes from the smoke. They burned like vinegar. Juan's hand reached the doorknob and began to turn it. Juliet's cries were piercing.

Barbara put her hand over Juliet's tiny mouth and nose and looked down into her reddish, brown eyes. Her cries began to subside.

Barbara turned away from the window to see Juan standing near the crib. The room was quiet now, the only sound Juan's heavy breathing.

Barbara took a step forward holding Juliet close to her body.

"There once was a village," she said. "And the village lived under the protection of a powerful being. To appease the being, every year the villagers had to make a sacrifice. It was considered a great honor."

Barbara turned back toward the window, and in an instant, her arms were empty.

November

THE SECRET CASTLE

Virginia Underwood

F ran glared at the felt skeleton still trying to wish her a Happy Halloween. Pulling the holiday interloper off of his hook, Fran took a deep breath and turned her key. She could have reached the house in half an hour any day of the week. But it was only once a year that she made the journey, the result of a carefully structured détente. They would come to her house for Christmas, on birthdays, everyone met at a restaurant, but for Thanksgiving, she bit the bullet and traveled home.

"Dad!" Fran called, the door opening halfway before stopping hard. "Dad! Mom! Anybody here?"

Putting her shoulder into it, she heard the crunch of collapsing cardboard, and the door opened enough for her to squeeze into the front hall. It was worse than last year, but she'd expected as much. Over the top of the boxes that blocked the doorway and traipsed up the font stairs peeked a framed portrait of ten-year-old Fran, draped with a ropey cobweb. With a heavy sigh, Fran pushed the hair back off of her forehead.

"Fran, is that you?" She heard her mother's voice somewhere deep within the house. "We're in the back."

Stepping over sloping piles of newspaper, shuffling around teetering stacks of boxes, Fran managed to slip through the pathway that led into the back of the house. Everything seemed to have a brownish-yellow tinge, the color of being forgotten. Behind the heaps, she could see flashes of wallpaper, the background of dull memories from her childhood before it disappeared. There was furniture in there, too. A wooden dining room set and china cabinet, a settee that belonged to her great-grandmother, an upright piano that occasionally plunked when a cat stepped on a key. The whole place had the faint smell of an unchanged diaper. As she weaseled her way into the kitchen, she saw her mother sitting at a table stacked high with papers and discarded plastic grocery bags. Her mother had cleared herself a spot to sit her cup and newspaper as if that little sliver were really all she could ever want.

"Franny!" Mother smiled. "You're here!"

"Hi, Mom." Fran kissed the soft powdery baby-skin of her mother's cheek. "Where's dad?"

"In the garden." Her mother replied, settling back into her chair. "He wanted to check on his lettuce before it gets dark."

"The house, Ma, it's…" Fran shook her head, struggling to find a word.

"I know, I know. It's all the stuff from the practice; we've got to have these files shredded. You can't just throw them in the trash." Her mother said, taking a sip from her mug. "And then there's all the stuff out of your grandmother's old house. We've got to go through it all."

"Dad shut down his practice six years ago." Fran sighed, looking around at the kitchen counters crowded with lopsided appliances and unpacked groceries. "I'll get you a shredder at Walmart."

"No, that would take forever, we've gotta call one of those shredding companies." Her mother said dismissively, "They're just expensive."

"Over six years you probably could have shredded it all by now." Fran watched her mother pick up her newspaper, drifting away as she usually did when the conversation turned this direction. "I'll pay for a shredding company if you need me to."

"Talk to your father about it," her mother shrugged, "it's his stuff."

With a shake of her head, Fran tramped through the kitchen into the back hallway where stacks of laundry overflowed onto the floor. Pushing aside a splay of wooden boards blocking the back door, she managed to muscle her way into the yard.

Taking a deep breath, she stood on the brick patio, the fragrant herbs that bordered the space letting loose their delicate scent in the late evening air. The green sweep of lawn beyond looked like it belonged in a decorating magazine, each blade of grass trimmed to the same exact height. Around the square of green were the beds, flawless in their lines; roses climbing wooden trellises on one side, a burst of wildflowers in the middle, and her father's vegetable garden on the far right. In the back center was the big oak, her old treehouse still nestled in its branches. Her castle, her father called it, her Secret Castle. From anywhere but the back garden, the treehouse was invisible, hidden by swathes of leaves. Armed with a camping lantern, sleeping bag, and battery-operated boombox, twelve-year-old Fran had abandoned her bedroom to her mother's ever-growing craft-supplies collection and moved into the treehouse. At first, her parents protested, but as with most things, their attention was quickly diverted. Until she graduated from high school, Fran lived in the treehouse, only returning inside when it was too cold to stay out. As she got older and bigger, she would wince each time she climbed the ladder, waiting for the sound of cracking wood. But it still seemed a better chance to take than staying in the house, where she always expected to be crushed in an avalanche of stuff.

"Dad," she called, "you out here?"

He emerged from his tool shed, pushing a baseball cap back on his head. "Hey," he motioned her over, "I thought that was you."

"The garden looks great," Fran said, as her father pulled her into a side hug. They stood for a moment looking down at the carefully tended row of lettuce heads. "But the house, Dad…"

"I know," he sighed, running a gloved hand under the brim of his hat, "we've got to get to work on it."

"Mom said a lot of it is old stuff from the practice."

"Probably," he nodded, leaning his shovel against the shed, "back when we thought you might take over we saved a lot of stuff."

She felt the stab in her gut that always came with mention of her taking over the practice, but she let it pass. With a deep breath, she looked up at the treehouse. "You been in lately?"

Her father shook his head. "I'm afraid the wood may be rotted out."

Probably, she thought to herself, you all have a way of letting houses rot. But it wasn't worth saying it out loud.

"Mom got a room fixed up for you," he pulled off his gloves. "Your old room."

"Really?" Fran was shocked to hear her mother made an effort. "That's nice of her. I've gotta get my bag out of the car. I think I'll go around the side gate."

"You need any help?" He asked as she started around the house.

"I'm fine," Fran called with a shake of her head, pausing at the corner to watch her father saunter back inside. Long and tall, he had the plain, hard-working nature of an Amish farmer. His years spent as a doctor while living in filth only scratched the surface of his contradictions. There was also his marriage to her mother, who could have played Mrs. Claus at shopping malls if she had not been busy keeping his medical practice running. Short and round, she was full of nervous energy. Her working life was efficient and practical, her personal life impulsive and dramatic. Fran was a hybrid capturing their incongruous nature.

Tall like her father, she carried weight like her mother. Even as her endocrinologist father ranted about diabetes, Fran and her mother grew ever heavier, racing each other to see who could do the most damage. Fran topped out at three-hundred and four-teen pounds when she was twenty-five, during her second year of medical school; the perfect reflection of her parents, a single embodiment of their own self-loathing.

But that was in the past. Fran did her breathing exercises on the way to the car. It always made her feel silly and transparent to do her breathing exercises in public, but she told herself it was ok to be fragile. It was ok to be vulnerable. Even if those feelings made her want to tear her hair out. It was ok.

Deep in a mental mantra, she almost collided with the jogger on the sidewalk.

"Whoa!" He side-stepped her at the last moment, "watch out, there."

Her first impulse was to tell him he ought to watch out, but then she caught sight of his smiling face, and a bubble of dread welled up in her throat. "Henry?"

"Hey, do we…" his brow knitted and he stopped bouncing his feet, "Fran?"

She was fifteen again, melting into the sidewalk on a hot summer day, wearing a pair of shorts that showed every lump of thigh and watching Henry Chambers jog down the street. Teenage Fran made a habit of soothing herself late at night by picturing his bare glistening chest until the spot between her legs ached with warmth. Seeing him now triggered a Pavlovian response, wiping her mind blank as her body fired on.

"Oh, yeah…" she shook her head clear, "I almost didn't rec-ognize you."

"You're one to talk." He grinned, "There's half as much of you."

"I guess so," she shrugged. It wasn't half, she reminded herself. It wasn't anywhere near half, and her goal was far less than that.

"You really look great. I mean it." He said. "You home for Thanksgiving?"

"Yah," she couldn't bring herself to look away from his grin, "you?"

"Just until Friday, then I've gotta get back. They've got me on call all weekend."

She nodded, gulping down the ball of spit that formed in her throat as he spoke. "I heard somewhere you're a doctor now. Facebook, maybe."

"Yeah, just finished my residency. It's kind of amazing. Did you ever end up going back...?"

"No," she shook her head, "I decided it wasn't for me."

"It's good you figured that out early," he said, his face woven with genuine concern. "Some people don't realize it until they get out there in practice and by then it's like it's too late."

Fran long suspected this might be the case with her father. While he seemed to love the academics of medicine, he was continually disgusted with his patients. As soon as the door closed behind them, he would rant about how poorly they cared for their health. How he simply could not see how people could live that way. She once asked him why he didn't stay on the faculty at the medical school and try for a tenured position. He launched into a litany of grievances about all the people there who had done him wrong, seeking to keep him from getting ahead. In the end, he decided it would serve them right if he skulked off to treat little old ladies who ate too many sweets. That would show them.

But Henry Chambers was nothing like her father. He was brimming with the clarity and focus her bloodline lacked; normal in all the best ways. He could have been a movie star if it weren't for the crook in his nose. His mousy brown hair, going grey at the temples, was cut in a short bristly crop. She looked down at his hands just long enough to obtain that he wasn't wearing a ring. "Well, it's good to see you." He touched her briefly on the shoulder, and she felt the spot throb. "How are your folks, by the way?"

It was a loaded question, though Henry didn't realize it, and she felt herself longing to let forth a tirade of secrets. "They're fine, the same as ever."

"Your dad still garden? I remember being a kid and finding any excuse to go back there. He'd let us pick tomatoes and watermelons in the summer. And he'd always give us apples for Halloween. They were so sweet, better than candy. I can still taste it."

"Yeah," she nodded. "Still gardening."

"Well," he looked her up and down again, "I'm glad to see you're doing so well."

"You, too."

"See you around," he waved, jogging on the few feet to his parents' house.

Feeling the blood return slowly to her limbs, Fran grabbed her bag out of the car and scurried back around the house. Dropping her belongings at the foot of the tree, she took hold of the wooden rungs leading up to the treehouse and held her breath. When the first one stayed, she seized the next, pulling herself up onto the creaky floor. The wood groaned a little, but the structure remained together. Next to the window that looked in the direction of the Chambers house was the box where she'd kept her old spy gear. Flipping the lid open with a bang, she was pleased to see that everything was where she'd left it. Blowing the dust off her binoculars, she aimed them at the Chambers house.

Between the leaves of the tree, she could see into their kitchen. Unlike her parent's home, no drapes were covering the windows or cardboard panels blocking out the light. His mother sat at the kitchen table glancing over a magazine, the only other items on its surface a pair of salt and pepper shakers. As she watched Mrs. Chambers turn the pages, Fran felt a lump in her throat grow larger; a longing to be in that house, sitting at that table. Henry entered through the living room, wiping sweat on his shirt, and got a glass of water. They spoke for a moment, she wondered if they were talking about her. Henry was probably telling his mother that he'd seen Fran outside, that she'd lost a lot of weight and looked really good. His mother was probably saying something about how she'd always liked Fran, and that he would be lucky to find a girl like her.

Henry picked his phone up from the counter where it was plugged into a charger. He leaned against the counter as he flipped through the screens. Fran was almost as enamored of Henry's family as she was of him. His sister was a lithe and pretty blonde, the former captain of the cheerleading squad, their father was one of those strong masculine types, decisive and firm; and his mother floated along, the perfect housewife, always ready with a smile and a cookie. If only she could have grown up in a house like that, maybe things would have been different for her.

Fran's phone buzzed in her pocket. She ignored it, probably some mass text message from someone she barely knew wishing everyone in their phone a Happy Thanksgiving! Then a dozen strangers would send back messages laced with inside jokes she didn't understand. The phone buzzed again, and Fran took it out of her pocket to turn it off when she stopped. Thumb hovering over the button, she saw the notification on her phone. Henry Chambers wants to be your friend! Heart thumping in her throat Fran gulped down air. She watched as Henry left the kitchen, disappearing for a moment, then reappearing upstairs in his corner bedroom, the same one he'd had when they were kids. She knew the bedroom like the back of her hand, although she'd never been inside. She imagined it smelled like dryer sheets and men's deodorant. The pungent flavor of teenage fantasies stuck in the back of her throat. Once again she slipped into a longing to lie on his blue-checkered bedspread and listen to Smashing Pumpkins cassettes, the way she'd always imagined romantic young couples did. But he was thinking of her, too, now. Maybe he had been thinking of her all along, waiting for her to find him again.

In the bedroom, he peeled off his sweaty shirt, the chest beneath only improving with age, broader and more developed than his youthful counterpart. He opened the door to the bathroom, loosening the string on his shorts.

"Fran!"

She jumped to hear her name, the binoculars dropping back into the box.

"Just a minute!" She called back to her mother. "I'll be right there."

"Where are you?" Her mother's voice was moving closer.

"I'm in the treehouse."

"In the treehouse! Get down from there before the whole thing falls in. It can't handle that much weight." Fran considered dead-dropping onto the old woman's head. With any luck, she'd kill them both. Instead, she began her breathing exercises. IN- one, two, three. OUT- one, two, three.

"Move out of the way," she said, her mother's scrunched face peering up the ladder, "I'm coming down."

Before hooking her foot onto the first rung, Fran looked down at her phone, with a deep breath she pushed the button. Accept!

Growing up, Fran assumed the house was always a mess because her parents were so busy with the practice. But since their retirement, neither had shown any indication of a desire to fix the place up. Her father puttered in the garden, her mother read newspapers and went shopping. Cleaning was something to be done tomorrow.

Out of the tree, Fran was led to her room by her mother. When the older woman proudly opened the door, Fran's heart dropped. "Oh." Fran glanced around. "It looks... nice."

The single bed was spread with a green quilt, and a tray table had been set up for her to use as a nightstand. A folding screen attempted to hide the mountain of stuff spilling out of the corner, a strategically placed chair guarding the boxes teetering on the other side. It was the most open space she'd yet encountered in the house. "Thanks, Mom." Fran smiled.

She sat down on the bed and looked at the top of the pile cresting over the screen. "What is all that stuff?"

"It's junk we tossed in here after we sold the old lake house." Her mother sighed, looking around. "We've got to go through it." When they sold the lake house, her mother told her they were doing it so they would have money to travel. Three years later and they hadn't been anywhere yet.

"I saw Henry Chambers outside," Fran glanced at her mother to check her expression, "he's a doctor now."

"I heard. His mom talks about it all the time." Fran's mother sighed, "Don't let it worry you. We're proud of you."

"I didn't mean it like that." Fran turned back to the pile, avoiding her mother's gaze.

"You've lost more weight," her mother broke the silence, "you're looking good."

"You, too," Fran said. "I can tell you've lost some."

Her mother's weight loss was the result of bariatric surgery. Fran's was the result of illogical determination. When her mother began to lose weight, it set off a nuclear arms race, each trying to lose the weight faster than the other. In spite of everything, they'd formed a bond over both being fat, and to be left behind alone on that island would have been heartbreaking.

"Does Dad have any apples?"

"Apples?" Her mother shrugged, "He's only got one tree now, but it should have some on it. Why?"

"I just thought I might take some to a friend." Fran opened her bag and fished out a lipstick.

"Are you taking them to Henry?" Her mother shifted a little in the doorway.

"Maybe," Fran said. "He mentioned he liked them; I thought it would be nice."

"You always were in love with the idea of that family," her mother sighed. "I remember when you were in high school; you were always going on about the Chambers. Why couldn't we be more like the Chambers? Well, I'll remind you that Mrs. Chambers has never worked. It's easy enough to have a perfect house when that's all you do."

"Sure," Fran rolled her eyes. "That's why."

"I don't remember you ever offering to do any chores."

"You're right, Mother," Fran said, feeling herself sink into a cold bath of disgust, "clearly I was the problem." She stood up and took a long look at the old woman's grimace before slamming the door.

Fran flipped through Henry's photos, letting her eyes sink into the bliss of his image. He was on a beach with another man, laughing into the glare of the sun; he was at a party, holding a cocktail and draped by a woman who clinked her glass against his; he was at the park with his Beagle, scrunching his nose as it tried to lick his face. He was living in a world full of perfect moments, dappled in just the right light, and Fran imagined how easy it would be to Photoshop herself into the picture. He didn't have a relationship status posted, and from what she could tell of his photos the dog was the most frequently recurring face.

In medical school, Fran would sit in front of her computer with the screen pulled up to Henry's profile. Willing herself to push the Friend Request button, she would always hesitate. What if he rejected it, or just never replied. She would stare at the thumbnail snap of his face and edge the mouse closer. But she never pushed the button. And now he had done it for her. Now she knew how he really felt.

There were many things Fran had learned to let go of in the years since her breakdown, but Henry Chambers was not one of them. Every time she looked at his picture, it was like pushing at the center of a bruise. As much as it hurt, she couldn't' help but want to do it again a few minutes later, pushing and pushing until the skin ruptured. Even though he may not know it yet, she understood they were destined to be together. It was only a matter of time, and she had waited, proved her fidelity. Now that she was smaller, he would be able to see it, too. He would usher her into a club of smiling, healthy people who shopped at Whole Foods and went kayaking on weekends. She would become an indispensable part of his world; his family would love her. They would all say to themselves how different she was from her parents; how it was amazing, she'd turned out so well.

Standing on the top step of his parent's front porch, she felt a rush of giddy anticipation, like a kid about to open presents when they already know what's inside. It was twilight, almost dark out, the temperature dropping fast. On the other side of the door, she could hear footsteps down a wooden hall.

"Coming!" Fran could hear Mrs. Chambers voice, light and delicate. The door swung open to a long, slender woman in a tidy shift dress holding a glass of wine. "Hello," Mrs. Chambers smiled, "I'm sorry, do we…"

"It's Fran, from next door." She felt herself blush. "I just wanted to bring Henry some apples." She held up the plastic shopping bag holding the fruit. "He mentioned he really liked them when I ran into him earlier."

"Fran!" Mrs. Chambers stepped aside and motioned her in, "I can't believe it! I never would have guessed it was you!"

"Thanks," Fran smiled, ducking her eyes down the hall. "I guess I've lost a little weight."

"Come on in," Mrs. Chambers stripped Fran out of her coat, leading her towards the living room. Fran could feel her head getting light. "Henry!" His mother called up the stairs. "Fran is here!"

In the living room, Mr. Chambers was sitting in an armchair reading a book and holding a crystal glass. Mrs. Chambers gestured for Fran to sit. "I'll take those." She said, reaching for the plastic bag. "Let me get you a drink. Wine alright?"

"Yes, thank you." Fran smoothed her skirt over her knees. "I brought Henry some apples." She said to Mr. Chambers when they were alone in the room together.

He offered a half-smile and a nod, "that's nice."

"Fran!" Henry appeared in the doorway wearing slacks and a blue V-neck sweater that showed off the cut of his shoulders. "I wasn't expecting to see you again so soon!"

"She brought you some apples," Mrs. Chambers reappeared, smiling into her full glass. "Wasn't that nice of her?"

"It really was," Henry nodded, offering Fran a conspiratorial grin.

"So," Mrs. Chambers sat down next to Fran on the sofa, handing her a glass of wine that Fran cupped in her open hands, "what's going on in your life Fran? Are you married? Any children?"

"No," Fran shook her head. "Nothing like that."

"You kids these days," Mrs. Chambers laughed and shook her head. She was remarkably beautiful for her age, the skin of her face still firm and smooth all the way down her graceful neck.

Mr. Chambers looked like he'd escaped from a 1960's sitcom, the rigidly attractive father who simmered with silent wisdom. "When we were coming along, people didn't wait so late to start a family."

"Oh great, here we go." Henry rolled his eyes. "Please don't start."

"I never thought I'd have two grown children and not a single grandchild. But a lot of things don't turn out how you expect them." She rolled her eyes over Henry. "Well, there are other things in life, I suppose. And look at Fran, doesn't she look nice," Mrs. Chambers lifted a lock of Fran's hair away from her face. "Don't you think she looks nice, Henry? She did bring you apples after all."

Fran was increasingly aware of the wine that Mrs. Chambers kept gulping down, the bourbon swishing in Mr. Chambers' glass.

"Mom, would you stop." Henry sighed. "You're embarrassing."

"I want grandchildren before I die!" Mrs. Chambers offered a dramatic fake pout. "That's all."

"My mom's always saying that, too." Fran smiled sheepishly, trying to lighten the mood. "I told her she's got a grand-dog and she should be happy with that."

Henry flashed a grateful smile as if they were in it together.

"I want a baby," Mrs. Chambers flapped a dismissive hand in the air, "a real live grandbaby. I keep thinking Karen will have one but she never does."

"Linda," Mr. Chambers gave off a low grumble, "knock it off."

"This is why Karen isn't here," Henry shook his head in disgust, "why do you think they always go to visit John's parents?"

"They're coming here for Christmas," Mrs. Chambers snapped, taking a slug from her glass. She bounced her crossed legs anxiously and waited for someone to speak. "You know

Henry's single, as well, Fran." Mrs. Chambers offered another grin, cutting her eyes towards her son. "You're not his usual type," Fran was lost in the joy of hearing her fantasy spoken out loud, "wouldn't it just be destiny if after all these years…"

"Mother!" Henry stood up. "That's not… appropriate."

"But think of all the apples you'd have, Henry." Mrs. Chambers snorted into her wine. "And maybe I'd finally get my grandchild. You'd have a baby with Henry for me, wouldn't you, Fran? Oh, Fran, of course, you would, you're such a good girl. Not like these flaky pretty boys my son can't seem to get enough of. He goes through them so fast it's not even worth learning their names. What was the last one, Henry? Darren or something…"

"Gavin." Henry corrected her. "Actually I'm still seeing him."

"Wait," Fran shook her head, "I don't understand…" While she knew the words, she had lost the meaning of them in the conversation. "Pretty boys?"

"Well yes, Henry's gay." Mrs. Chambers was grinning from ear to ear; her perfect alabaster skin flushed rosy with wine. "Didn't you know?"

"Gay." Fran felt her heart drop down her throat and into her stomach, hands unable to grip the wineglass that tipped forward into her lap. "Gay?"

All of the family members rushed for the kitchen at the same time, returning with various cloths to pat Fran's pants dry. "Let me put some club soda on it," Mrs. Chambers was saying, "I think club soda works."

Blood rushed from the top of Fran's head to the bottom of her legs, the world erupting into spinning stars. Breaths came shallow and fast as she urged her lungs to keep up with her racing heart. Now they were all touching her, hovering over her with their perfect catalog-model bodies; pushing in on her with their drunken shock and pseudo-concern.

"I'm fine!" She jumped up, tugging down the hem of her shirt. "I'm fine, ok. I think I should leave."

"Fran," Henry was saying, "I'm sorry…"

"I didn't realize you didn't know." Mrs. Chambers said, offering a forlorn look to the empty glass. But now Fran saw. She understood the knowing grin and the way Mrs. Chambers had chuckled at the apples. As if it wasn't funny enough that Fran was interested in Henry, she didn't know.

"Why do you have to do things like this?" Henry turned on his mother. "What's wrong with you?"

Fran slipped into her coat, Henry's parents returning to their bar. "Do we have to do this now," Mrs. Chambers was rolling her eyes, "you always get so worked up about every little thing."

Without a sound, Fran slid onto the front stoop, leaving the door open behind her. Outside the neighborhood was the same as ever. Cars parked along the road, trees swaying in a slight breeze, living rooms full of reunited loved-ones lit up as beacons against the dark. Her breaths were coming back to her as jagged rips that hung in white clouds before her face. When she was on the sidewalk, she heard the door close, a pair of sneakers on the steps.

"Fran!" Henry called. He was jogging towards her, wearing a camel pea coat and a green scarf that matched his eyes. His face was rosy and vibrant in the cold air. "Hey wait a second. Look, I'm sorry about all that."

"It's ok," she shook her head. "I didn't mean to cause any problems…"

"It wasn't your fault," he shrugged, "my Mom, she took it hard when I came out. She wants me to be someone I'm not."

She nodded and chewed the inside of her cheek, fighting back a stream of angry tears.

"I wanted to say thanks for the apples, too. It was really sweet of you to think of me." He was picture perfect. This is where snow should have started to fall, where they would have had their first kiss. "And look, I don't know… I mean, I'm sorry that you found out that way, I didn't even think about it, I've been out for a while now, I just figured you knew."

"I didn't know. I had no idea." She managed to squeak.

"Really?" He shook his head. "I didn't mean to upset you or anything. I know the holidays can't be easy, being here with your parents and all."

"What?" She felt the tears halt in their ducts, the churning hot spot in her belly release. "What do you mean?"

"Well, because of the house." He shrugged a shoulder towards her parent's place. "You know, 'cause they're hoarders. I mean the whole neighborhood knows, even though they try to hide it. It can't be easy to deal with that."

Everything inside of her went still. Feeling her heartbeat slow and breathing become smooth, she focused her stone eyes on his innocent grin.

"You're disgusting," she said, the words coming out as a whisper at first, "I've never met anyone more revolting in my entire life."

"What are you talking about?" His expression melted into confusion.

"You think you're so goddamn adorable," she snarled, "but you're just another disgusting little slut. You're just another boring, basic little bitch. You're so full of shit! And everyone knows it. They may not say it out loud, but they know. They think you're just as dirty as I do. Your parents, your friends, your co-workers, even your patients. They can see your filth; they know your secret. And once they know your secret, they never think of you the same way again. It'll always be there," her face followed his up the sidewalk, pressing him into a fence post, "They'll always think of you as the nasty little queer boy, no matter how hard you try to be one of the guys. 'Cause you aren't. They'll think you're just as despicable as I do, but they won't do you the favor of saying it out loud."

"You're fucking crazy!" He yelled, pushing her back.

"Run away, you scared little freak boy," she hissed, "You're fucking revolting to me now."

With a shove she sent him scampering back to his parent's house. "You're a crazy bitch!" He screamed from the top step. "You stay away from me, or I'll call the police!"

Fran marched the short distance back to her parent's, throwing herself against the door. In the front room, her mother and father sat in their respective recliners, a TV tray with the remains of dinner in each one's lap. A third chair waited for her, the spot where she would usually eat her Thanksgiving meal.

A stack of books nestled each recliner into its own cubby, a leaning tower of old medical texts and bargain-bin detective novels. "How did it go at the Chambers?" Her mother asked, cast in blue light by the flickering TV. Fran noticed that the old woman was getting jowly. "Did he ask you to marry him?"

"What?" Fran stood over her mother's chair. Her father's eyes were still fixed on the screen. "What did you say?"

"Oh Fran," mother sighed with a wave of her hand, "I'm just joking with you. Everyone knows he's flaming gay."

With blood pounding in her ears Fran drew in a long, slow breath. One-two-three. She felt the cloud descending over her head, a soundless euphoria. One-two-three. Unprompted her legs were carrying her through the house, out the back, and into the garden. One-two-three. Fran looked up at the Secret Castle, standing cold and silent in the trees. One-two-three.

Uncertain of just how she arrived in the treehouse, Fran found herself back at her spy window. Lifting the binoculars to her eyes, she focused them on the Chambers house. Downstairs she could just see Mr. and Mrs. Chambers in the living room, still sipping their drinks. Henry was upstairs in his room sitting on the end of his bed, tears streaming down his face. Fran opened the door and stepped inside, sitting down next to him at the end of the bed.

I'm sorry, she said. I shouldn't have said that.

Oh, Fran. He took her hand, buried his face in her neck. I'm sorry, too. I was just afraid to tell you the truth. Their lips hovered inches apart, the heat of his breath warming her skin. It's always been you.

Something beneath her gave out a shattering groan, and before Fran could find the source of the noise, the floor was sliding forward. Bracing herself against the window frame she fell, the earth jumping up to meet the side of the Secret Castle, the slope of the splintered branch breaking the fall just enough that Fran tumbled out of the open window and rolled onto the green lawn, looking up at the night sky. For a moment she lay in perfect stillness, to her side the treehouse looked back at her from where it also lay on its side, equally dazed.

The back door burst open, and her parents were running towards her. She could hear their voices growing louder, though they still seemed far away.

"Fran!" Her mother was screaming, falling at her daughter's side. "Fran are you ok?!"

Her father took up each of Fran's hands, bending the fingers back and forth, then pulled off her socks to do the same with her toes. He drew his penlight from his top pocket and shone it into her eyes, sending Fran twitching away. "Does anything hurt?" He asked.

"Not really." Fran sighed. "I don't think so."

"Fran, are you ok?" Her mother asked again.

"Huh?" Fran looked at her, sitting up on her elbows, "Yes, I'm ok."

"I told you that treehouse couldn't handle that much weight." Mother sighed, standing up and extending a hand to Fran.

Fran nodded as her mother pulled her to her feet, and she leaned into the old woman's soft side.

"Let's get you ready for bed. You've gotta get up early to help me with the casseroles. Your father can work on getting this mess picked up tomorrow." Mother sighed, giving the remains of the Secret Castle a final glance. "Anyway, it was time for it to come down. It was dangerous."

A HOSTAGE OF PENTHOS

Steven Sanders

A winter storm of snow and ice obscures anything low to the ground—even the bodies of the dead—and storms are in the forecast.

Evan Shipman lays awake in his bed, the first blue glow of morning lighting his room. He glances at the clock by his bed and groans. The room is cold, but he stands and staggers to the window and lifts the sash, shivering as the blast of freezing air shocks him awake. His eyes sting, and his head is conflicted, a mixture of anticipation and irritation, pleased by the harbingers of winter outside—frost on the trees, snow buntings on the ground—but riled by the unwelcome morning and the noisy kids outside shouting and running for the bus stop. The clock by his bed shows 6:56 AM, and he has not slept all night.

From: Dr. Robert Ellis <r.ellis@vatech.edu>
Sent: Thursday, December 1, 2017 9:10 AM
To: Dr. Evan Shipman <eshipman@virginia.edu>
Subject: Insomnia

Hey Ship. I got your voicemail. Good to hear from you. Hey we need to get together over the holidays. It's been too long. How are things at UVA these days? I imagine there's quite a cloud hanging over campus since August.

Anyway, glad you liked the article. Yes, the essential premise is that in pre-industrial agrarian societies bi-phasic sleep was predominant, demonstrated by many dozens of references in Western lit, court records, letters, diaries, etc. to "first sleep" and "second sleep" and in between those a waking period of 1-3 hours in the middle of the night. So maybe we've been doing it wrong for centuries.

Still, I'm reluctant to recommend you start going to bed every night at dark. I know insomnia is tough to live with. Have you seen a doctor? With all you've been through, it can't be easy. Hang in there old pal. Things will get better. -Rob

In a row of handsome brick offices on the outskirts of McLean, Virginia, Shipman sits back in a deep leather armchair, waiting for his doctor to stop talking. He ignores the walnut bookcase lined with vintage textbooks and leather-bound editions selected to impress. His attention drifts as he stares out a bay window at a sky gray as gunmetal. On the edge of a wooded park, he notices the few pale orange leaves fluttering on the limbs of a beech tree, the last in a stand of hardwoods to hold its foliage. Soon they too will fall and freeze.

"The point is you shouldn't be discouraged. Most people go through it at some point in their lives."

Shipman turns his head, his attention back inside the office. "Most people go through what?"

"Insomnia. It's usually short-term."

Short-term. Such an imprecise phrase. "How do you define that? Weeks? Months?"

"I said *usually*. Insomnia, anxiety, depression… it can be all be more intense during the holidays. Which is why we should consider a different medication. I think it's the best course."

"Well I don't." Shipman shakes his head. "I'm done with the drugs."

"The side-effects will subside."

"Jack, it doesn't matter. I'm thinking of something different."

"Such as?"

Shipman sighs and turns his eyes back to the window. "A colleague from my former life published an interesting article last month."

"What kind of article?"

"Sleep patterns through history."

"Okay."

"Essentially he says throughout human pre-history, people went to sleep when the sun went down."

"Pre-history… as in cave men?"

"Early pre-humans, prehistoric hunter-gatherers."

"Well, I'm sure cavemen and hunter-gatherers got pretty exhausted from all that hunting and gathering. It's no wonder they went to sleep when the sun went down."

"Right. So they would sleep a few hours. Then they would wake in the middle of the night for a few hours, then go back to sleep until sunrise. He calls it 'segmented sleep.'"

"I see. And they woke up in the middle of the night? What did they do?"

"Normal things. Stoke the fire, eat, pray, have sex. In recent centuries read if they could. Then go back to sleep until sunrise. The theory is that human beings evolved over millions of years sleeping that way, two separate blocks. And only in the last couple of hundred years or so, we started sleeping in a single block of seven or eight hours. Since the industrial revolution and electric lights. And what we now think of as insomnia is just a side-effect because our modern way of sleeping is actually *unnatural*."

"Well... unnatural is a strong word, Ship. And it sounds a little strange."

"I'll send you the article. A man in your line of work should know this stuff."

"Have you been drinking?"

"No. But I'm anxious to start back."

PROGRESS NOTES

Date:	*12/1/17*
Patient:	*Evan Shipman*
DOB:	*10/11/1974*
DX:	*Chronic sleep maintenance insomnia secondary to generalized anxiety disorder, depression, alcoholism*
Rx:	*Eszopiclone 3 mg one tab qhs*
Notes:	*Pt. C/O continued difficulty sleeping, night terrors, frequently awakens in confusion and panic. Resulting fatigue, difficulty concentrating @ work, agitation with students, colleagues. Presents w/ low-grade psychomotor retardation. Mood agitated. Reports medication leaves him impaired the following morning/day. Discussed altering meds but pt. disagreed. Prior rx: zolpidem also caused unwanted s/e, discontinued use 6/17. During session patient described historical journal article describing "segmented sleep" as a more natural pattern of sleep in line w/ circadian rhythms. Pt. proposes to transition to sleep segmented by 2-3 hour awake. Pt. was advised against this as it is at odds with accepted protocol and will inhibit evening social interactions, increase time spent withdrawn, excessive solitude, likely aggravating depression, anxiety, agitation, alcohol abuse.*
	—J. Martinson, MD

•　　　•　　　•　　　•

As the afternoon fades, Shipman drives southwest from McLean for two hours. He listens to a Christmas oratorio for distraction, but when the news comes on, he switches the radio off. Traffic is heavy until he passes some invisible line where the DC suburbs end and the hillbilly country begins. Only for Jack would he venture so close to the beltway. There was a time when he lived and worked in the capital, within the system, inside the "halls of power." No more. Now the 30-mile drive to UVA in Charlottesville four days a week is as far as he wants to go, as close as he cares to get to the bacterial infection in the capital, the clown show on Pennsylvania Avenue. He drives in the opposite direction, past Madison, Shelby, Boonesville, small towns, and each smaller than the last, until he passes the forest preserve. Low mountains rise to the west, and the road narrows, crowded by red maple trees, white birch, and yellow poplars. He crosses Doyle's River, icy water rushing beneath the bridge, and passes Montfair Farm lit up with Christmas lights, and at last turns onto Old Ice Pond Road.

Along this little lane, hidden among the hills and the evergreens, are three miniature lakes, so small nobody has bothered giving them names. Beyond the lakes lies the Shenandoah forest. Shipman's house sits on a hill, tucked into the trees overlooking the northernmost lake.

He stops the car and watches two boys on the lakeshore testing the ice. Behind them a nervous fawn looks from the edge of the pine woods. She has grown fast in six months, and her white spots have turned now to tan. Where is her mother?

An hour after sunset, Shipman goes to his bed, his stomach still pleasantly full from a pan-seared ribeye and a bottle of syrah. He rubs his eyes and turns off the bedside lamp. The pillow is soft on his cheek, and soon his head turns foggy. In his mind he sees the fawn again. She stands alone in the meadow between the trees and the frozen pond, light and airy with her ears pricked up and eyes shining at him. For a moment he isn't sure whether he's awake or asleep.

Forty minutes later he is up and alert again, staring at the blue digits on his bedside clock: 6:52 PM. His mind leaps from one worry to another. Final exams. Student evaluations. Tenure. The mortgage. The ladder. The point? At 7:43 PM he hears a noise in the hallway. He gets up and switches a light on but finds nothing. At 8:17 PM he turns on the bedside lamp and reads from David McCullough's *John Adams*. He finds it tiresome and turns off the light at 8:53 PM. The noise again, like something whining. He goes out, but it's not in the hallway. Something outside the hallway window? He looks out but sees nothing but the evergreens bending in the breeze.

He returns to bed and stays there for ten more hours. He does not sleep.

From: Dr. Jacob Martinson MD <r.martinson@valley.com>
Sent: Friday, December 2, 2017 7:10 AM
To: Dr. Evan Shipman <eshipman.@virginia.edu>
Subject: Sleeping

Good morning Ship. I wanted to check and see how it went last night. Hope you got some sleep. Call me at work.

-Jack

At 11:33 AM, Shipman looks over a crowd of students. "One minute," he says.

Scattered gasps pervade the lecture hall as the herd of privileged millennials frantically scribbles their last recitations on the impacts of the Fugitive Slave Act of 1850 and how paper currency inflation shattered the Southern financial infrastructure during the U.S. Civil War.

"Time," Shipman says. "Stop writing and pass your exams forward." He looks down at a young man wearing a parka and flip-flops, still scrawling in his booklet. "Now," says Shipman.

PROGRESS NOTES

Date:	*12/2/17*
Patient:	*Evan Shipman*
DOB:	*10/11/74*
DX:	*CSM insomnia secondary to generalized anxiety, depression, alcoholism*
Rx:	*N/A*
Notes:	*Pt. returned my message regarding the first night of his "segmented sleep" experiment. Apparently it didn't go well. Restless, agitated most of the night. Estimates he slept less than one hour. Set next appt for 12/14. Will revisit medication.*
	—J. Martinson, MD

On the drive home, Shipman stops at a dollar store and buys a dozen large candles. The old woman at the register smiles at him.

"Getting ready for the lights to go out?"

"Something like that," Shipman replies.

"Lord, I hope not. Awful early for a winter storm. I just hope there ain't no ice." She rings up the sale and hands him the bag with a smile. "You stay warm now, you hear?"

By three o'clock, Shipman has been splitting wood for almost an hour. With each heavy swing, his axe ruptures an oak log, its cleaved chunks flying in opposite directions. In the yard nearby, firewood is piled four feet high. Shipman's shirt is wet with sweat, and when he stops to sharpen the axe blade, he gets a chill. The temperature is below twenty degrees when the school bus rounds the lane, its brakes hissing. The kids from down the road jump out and head home different directions. Two boys run down the hill toward the lake. They are laughing and shouting, and the smaller boy takes a tumble on the frozen ground. They reach the shore and immediately test the ice, pushing down with one foot while keeping the other on the bank. Shipman waits and watches as they inch out onto the ice, further and further from the bank.

"Get off there!" Shipman marches across the road and down the hillside. "Hey! You kids stay off that lake!"

"Hey leave us alone," a boy squeaks. "We ain't doin' nothing."

As Shipman nears, the boys look alarmed. They take a step back and glance quickly at each other, mouths half open. Shipman stops and realizes he's still holding the axe in his left hand.

"Look," he says. "I don't want you boys out on that ice. It's not safe. Now get off there."

The boy farthest out stands and stares back a moment in a show of strength. "No."

"Boy, I'm not asking you a question."

The boy swears and steps lightly across the ice to solid ground.

"Now get on home before I call your parents."

Later as the snow falls, Shipman carries an armful of split logs into the house and piles them by the fireplace in the den. He sits on the raised brick hearth and piles wood into the firebox. The wood is dry, seasoned a year, and he stacks it up like a pyramid, with large logs at the base and layers of smaller and smaller wood rising up. At the top, he lays kindling then tinder. He lights the fire with a single match.

Shipman takes a stepladder from a closet and sets it up in the middle of the room. He climbs onto the third step, reaches up to the light fixture on the ceiling, unscrews and removes the light bulbs. He takes the ladder and repeats the task in the kitchen, the dining room, and every other room on the first floor. Then he does the same with the second floor and the basement. Incandescent bulbs, halogen bulbs, spiral CFLs, LEDs—soon every bulb from every light fixture, lamp, and sconce in the house—along with every clock—is packed away in cardboard boxes and stowed in the garage.

The only room he avoids is the small bedroom at the end of the hallway upstairs. Even in the gloom, the door shines with colorful stickers and crayon drawings—the door he hasn't entered in more than 11 months.

Shipman goes to his bedroom and removes his wristwatch, but it's too dark to see the inscription on steel. He puts it on the dresser and looks out the window. Outside the snow is falling.

He gropes toward the glow from the den, where flames are leaping in the fireplace and brightening the room. He eats a little supper in front of the fire and falls asleep in the den, the couch pulled up close by the fireplace. He does not sleep straight through the night, but much of it, and the times awake are well-spent adding wood and stoking the fire. The room is warm and soothing, and ghosts do not disturb him when he stares into the flames.

●   ●   ●   ●

Twelve days later, Shipman sits in the leather chair across from the doctor.

"So it's working for you? This...segmented sleep?"

Shipman nods. "Yes, it is."

"Just like that?"

"No, not just like that. It took some adjusting. I'm still adjusting, I think. "

"But you still wake up a lot?"

"Well nothing's perfect, Jack. But it's helping. I mean, my God I feel so much better already. My head is clearer. Do you know what it's like not to sleep for days? It's a hell of a lot better than those damn pills you gave me."

"Okay, I get it."

"And the dreams. You wouldn't believe the dreams I have. So vivid, full of colors and weird things. And I remember my dreams because I wake up in the night, and they're just—there."

"So explain the process. What time do you turn in?"

"I try to have some dinner while it's still light out."

"So that's what...four o'clock?"

"Closer to five. And then I start winding down and go to bed maybe an hour later."

"But this time of year, it's dark nearly fifteen hours a day. That's too much sleep."

"I'm not sleeping fifteen hours a day, Jack. It's more like eight or nine. You're exaggerating everything."

"Sorry. It's just all so—"

"Strange? I know. It's strange to me too."

"But keep in mind, insomnia isn't the only thing to be concerned about here, Ship. There's also the anxiety, the depression."

"I'm not depressed."

"No? The semester's over, and you're withdrawing like some kind of a hermit. You don't get out. Christmas is two weeks away, and you're not even going home."

"I'm not facing that family again. That would be depressing."

"You can't stay away forever."

"Why not?"

"It's where you grew up. Your family is there."

"No. *Her* family is there. My family is gone."

A long silence. An impasse.

"What about the alcohol? Have you been drinking?"

"I got a little drunk the first night. Since then not as much."

"You shouldn't be drinking at all."

"Oh shut up. You know, all that crap about stopping drinking is just bullshit. Your profession thinks everybody's an alcoholic and the only way to deal with it is cold turkey. How does that usually work out? Isn't the AA success rate like seven percent? I told you, I'm not drinking much. I'm getting exercise, and I'm sleeping for the first time in a year. I'm actually doing well, no thanks to you. Why am I even here? What am I paying you for?"

"You don't pay me. That's why you're here."

"Right." Shipman sighs and nods. "I'm not used to being a sponge."

"You never let me buy you anything since freshman year. Even a beer. This is the least I can do."

Shipman grins. "That's for sure, you rich bastard."

"Yeah, well... You're not poor."

"Not anymore."

"And I could lose my license just for treating you. Asshole."

"Well, at least I'm off your damn pills, so you're not liable for that insanity anymore."

"You mentioned your dreams. What are you dreaming about?"

"You're gonna analyze my dreams now, Dr. Freud?"

"Come on."

"Jesus Christ." Shipman takes a breath and looks toward the ceiling. "Well, let's see. Trees. Woods. Deer. I dream about deer a lot. Deer creeping around the house. Around the lake. The weather is always cold. Sometimes there's a blizzard. The lake is frozen. I'm skating on the lake."

"But it's not a nightmare?"

"No, it's not a nightmare. Just a very vivid dream."

"Really?"

"You sound surprised."

"Well, when someone suffering from anxiety and night terrors says his dreams are more vivid and memorable than ever..."

"Look, I know where you're going with this, and I know it's strange."

"That's the second time you've admitted all this is strange."

"Well it is. I am aware of that."

"Well, I'm glad it seems to be working for you."

"Thank you."

"So… I guess you made it through the storm okay?"

Storm? Shipman has to think back. "Yeah, fine. You?"

"Not too bad. We stayed in for a couple of days, so it was sort of like a camping trip. The girls had fun." The doctor pauses. "So you're not using any lights at all?"

Shipman shakes his head. "Just firelight and candles."

"Jesus. Your house must look like a mausoleum."

Shipman shrugs.

"Well, be careful and don't accidentally burn the place down."

PROGRESS NOTES

Date:	*12/14/2017*
Patient:	*Evan Shipman*
DOB:	*10/11/74*
DX:	*CSM insomnia sec to gen. anxiety, depression, alcoholism*

PROGRESS NOTES

Rx:	*N/A*
Notes:	*Office visit. Patient reports decreased sleep latency, improved sleep maintenance. Increased exercise e.g. chopping wood, hiking. Removed all artificial lighting, uses only a few candles for light after dark. Shut off furnace. Heating house only by fire. Goes to bed approx. one hour after sunset. Sleeps soundly until around midnight. Rises for 2-3 hours, reads by candlelight, plays piano, writes in journal, goes for hikes/walks if moonlight permits. Reported hiking 12 miles in the middle of the night during full moon 12/4. Reports improved mental clarity, mood is improved but defensive when questioned about his habits. Has not left home for over a week until today. Admits resumption of alcohol use but insists he doesn't drink to excess. Physical appearance: unshaven, clothes more casual (due to end of semester?).*
	—J. Martinson, MD

On the drive home, Shipman stops to buy a few things.

"Did you lose power during the storm?" asks the old woman at the register.

"Excuse me?"

"You're buying more of them big candles like the last time you was here. Just reckoned you lost power during the ice storm."

"Oh right. The storm."

"Yes sir. I never seen nobody go through candles like you, sir."

●   ●   ●   ●

PROGRESS NOTES

Date:	*12/15/2017*
Patient:	*Evan Shipman*
DOB:	*10/11/74*
DX:	*CSM insomnia 2nd anx., dep., alc.*
Rx:	
Notes:	*Did some online research today. Found 1992 study in Jrnl Sleep Research by T. Wehr re: photoperiodocity. Subjects living in darkness 14 hrs/ day without artificial light transition (revert?) to "biphasic" sleep averaging 7-9 hours but separated by 2-3 hours awake. During waking interval subjects fully alert/lucid w/ sense of calm. Onset of sleep concurrent with spike in melatonin secretion triggered by darkness. Study suggests biphasic sleep tendency aka segmented sleep was pervasive prior to industrial rev. and onset of electric lighting. I must admit Ship may have stumbled upon something here. This study seems to back up his claims.*
	—J. Martinson, MD

On the night of the solstice, a soft snow falls after sunset, gently dusting the trees and hills in white silence. By the time Shipman wakes at midnight, the stands of spruce along the lake have gathered a fine powder in their boughs. The clouds clear out, and behind a waxing crescent moon, the stars shine like the heads of nails hammered to hold up the sky. Shipman walks down to the shore in bare feet, stands in the snow, and listens to the eerie high humming noise as the water freezes on the surface of the lake.

After he returns to bed, dreams rush in. He is skating on the lake, gliding in figure eight patterns across the ice. From the hillside, the fawn looks on, and this time her mother stays beside her in the snow.

• • • •

From: Dr. Robert Ellis <r.ellis@vatech.edu>
Sent: Thursday, December 22, 2017 9:10 AM
To: Evan Shipman <eshipman.@virginia.edu>
Subject: New Year's Eve!

Hey Ship. Just a quick FYI that Jill and I are having a little
holiday party New Year's Eve and you gotta get up here buddy!
Nothing too crazy but I've got a new reserve bourbon you
need to try. About seven here at the house. You know the way.
It's been too long, so don't bail on me. —Rob

"Ship, you have to get out more."

Shipman stares out the window. "I'm fine."

"You're not fine."

Frost clings to the window pane, and outside the snowy
parking lot is almost empty.

"You didn't seem too concerned the last time I was here."

"I didn't think you'd keep it up this long."

"Maybe you don't know me as well as you thought."

"What are you doing with your time?"

"Reading. Writing. Stoking the fire. I taught myself
Beethoven's Moonlight Sonata. Except for the third movement.
Don't think I'll get that part."

"When was the last time you left the house?"

"I leave the house almost every night."

"I don't mean stalking around in the middle of the night.
When was the last time you got out and did something with
other people?"

"When was I here last?"

"It's not funny, Ship. Why don't you come over to the house
this weekend?"

"Definitely not up for that."

"Do you really want to be alone on Christmas?"

"Don't you think I deserve to be?"

"Don't say things like that."

"It's a gift actually. Sometimes life gives us these moments of utter clarity."

PROGRESS NOTES

Date:	*12/22/2017*
Patient:	*Evan Shipman*
DOB:	*10/11/74*
DX:	*Insomnia sec to anxiety, depression, alcoholism*
Rx:	*N/A*
Notes:	*Pt reports improved sleep maintenance, but his appearance is alarming, unshaven, clothes not clean, visible weight loss. Lucid but distant, sarcastic. Reported bizarre behavior, trekking through the woods between "first sleep" and "second sleep" hunting at night and taking "cold air baths" i.e. standing naked outside his house in the freezing air in middle of the night. Unusual behavior becoming more pronounced as first anniversary of family deaths nears. Concerned he may become a danger to himself.*

It's nearly dark when Shipman arrives at home. He glances toward the lake, but nobody is there. The boys are outside playing some game in the road. Inside the house, Shipman lights a candle, goes to the garage, and rummages through some old boxes. After a minute or two, he comes across the object of his search: a pair of ice skates, black leather, men's size 11.

PROGRESS NOTES

Date:	*12/24/17*
Patient:	*Evan*
DOB:	
DX:	
Rx:	
Notes:	*Further research at home re: photoperiodocity and biphasic sleep. 2007 study Univ. Helsinki by Galvite and Meri reports subjects living in darkness 14+ hrs/day reported improved rest via segmented sleep but a smaller subset ~7% unexpected combination of calm mood with nonpar. delusions during waking segment, EEG brain waves display altered state of cons. differing from ordinary waking, REM or deep sleep, theta state analogous to trance, hypnosis, sleepwalking, degrading to depressive psychosis, cause/s undetermined.*

The crescent moon is barely a sliver in the sky as Shipman glides across the frozen lake. With nothing to obstruct his path, he stares up at the stars and skates a long, looping path over the ice, again, again, again. The ice hisses beneath the blades. His legs are powerful pistons, and he pushes himself faster and faster until his lungs gasp, and his quads burn with acid, but his mind is far way until he feels the uneven places where the ice is cracking under his feet.

●   ●   ●   ●

Body of UVA Professor Discovered in Frozen Lake Where Wife and Child Died a Year Ago

By Claudia Snow

December 27, 2017

CROZET—The body of a University of Virginia professor was discovered Tuesday partially frozen in an icy lake in rural Albemarle County, the same lake where his wife and daughter drowned on Christmas Eve a year ago.

Dr. Evan M. Shipman was found by three youths around 12 p.m., according to a statement released by Albemarle Sheriff Jim Stocker. Emergency services were alerted just after 12:30 p.m. The 43-year-old widower was pronounced dead at the scene at 1:48 p.m.

The unnamed lake is across the road from Shipman's home in the northwest corner of the county bordering Shenandoah National Park.

Shipman was a professor of U.S. History specializing the Civil War, according to the UVA faculty and staff web page. Witnesses reported having seen him skating on the frozen lake recently late at night and in the early morning hours.

Shipman's wife Natalie Colby Shipman, 36, and daughter Shelby Harper Shipman, 6, died under similar circumstances on the afternoon of December 24, 2016, when they fell through the ice while skating on the same lake. Shipman also broke through the ice that day but was rescued by emergency first responders.

Daytime temperatures in the area have been in the twenties most of December, but on December 24 the official high in Crozet was 45 degrees.

From: Dr. Robert Ellis <r.ellis@vatech.edu>
Sent: Wednesday, December 27, 2017 9:11 AM
To: Dr. Evan Shipman <eshipman.@virginia.edu>
Subject: New Year's Eve!

Hey Ship. Just checking back about NYE. Hope you can make it. We've been wondering how you're doing. I'm sure Christmas wasn't easy. Did you ever see anyone about the insomnia? Modern medicine is amazing. Don't be afraid to give it a try.

—Rob

Office of the Medical Examiner
1127 Court Street
Charlottesville, Virginia

Postmortem Examination	*12/28/2017; 8:30 A.M.*
Examiner	*Gregory Arnold, M.D.* *327 Miller Avenue, Arlington, VA* *661-234-1287 (FAX 661-234-1288)*

SUMMARY REPORT

Name:	*SHIPMAN, Evan Michael*
Coroner's Case #	*2017-12551*
Date of Birth	*10/11/1974*
Age	*43*
Race	*White*
Sex	*Male*
Date of Death	*12/25/2017*
Body Identified By	*Dr. Jacob Martinson, MD, McLean VA*
Investigative Agency	*Albemarle Sheriff's Department*
Medical Treatment	*N/A*
External Examination	*Post-rigor body is presented in a black body bag. The victim is wearing black sweatpants, gray wool socks, black ice skates. The only jewelry is a silver wedding band on left fourth finger.* *The body is that of a normally developed white male, HT 73 inches, WT 178.5 LBS, appearing generally consistent with the stated age of 43 years. The body is cold and unembalmed.*

External Examination, Cont.	*The eyes are open. The irises are blue and corneas are clear. The pupils measure 0.3 cm. The hair is dark brown with some gray at the temples and 1-2 inches in length.*
	Visible skin maceration due to water immersion. Multiple abrasions to both hands. Multiple abrasions on both forearms. A minor laceration is present on the R forefinger, and the L thumb has a purple contusion beneath the nailbed. Limbs are equal, symmetrically developed and show no evidence of injury.
	Residual 1" scar on R shoulder consistent with gunshot wound. Residual 3" scar on R lower abdomen consistent with appendectomy. Residual 1" scar below right eye. Residual 3" scar to R knee consistent with ACL surgery. Residual 2" scar at base of R thumb.
	No other markings or tattoos.
INTERNAL EXAMINATION	
Head/CNS	*The brain weighs 1,423 grams within normal limits.* *The sphenoid sinuses contain approximately 6 ml of fluid.*
	EVIDENCE OF DROWNING
Skeletal System	*Unremarkable.*

Respiratory System	*R lung 455 grams; L lung 462 grams.*
	Lungs display emphysema aquosum. Plural surfaces marbled, dark red linked to collapsed alveoli. Lung parenchyma pink to dark red, firm, congested.
	EVIDENCE OF DROWNING.
Cardiovascular System	*Heart grossly normal. Weight 353 grams. Normal configuration. No evidence of infarction or atherosclerosis. Pericardium intact. Epicardial fat diffusely firm.*
	No TTC staining utilized as pt. was postmortem > 48 hours. Slightly raised white plaques in the left ventricle wall lining. Ventricles unremarkable.
	Aorta: Minimal atherosclerosis with no measurable plaques along the full length of the ascending and descending aorta.
Gastrointestinal System	*The mucosa and wall of the esophagus are intact and gray-pink, without lesions or injuries. The gastric mucosa is intact and pink without injury.*
	Approximately 125 ml of partially digested semisolid food in the stomach. The mucosa of the duodenum, jejunum, ileum, colon and rectum intact.
Urinary System	*Kidneys L 123 grams, R 121 grams, anatomic in size, shape and location and without lesions.*

Genital System	*No injuries or abnormalities.*
Toxicology/Serology	*R pleural fluid, blood, and bile samples submitted for toxicology analysis. Stomach contents saved.*
Laboratory Data	*Cerebrospinal fluid culture and sensitivity: Unremarkable* *Gram stain: Unremarkable* *Drug Screen Results: Negative* *Blood alcohol: Negative* *Urine screen/immunoassay: Negative* *Ethanol: 0 gm/dl, Blood (Heart)* *Millicent Schmidt, Ph.D.* *Chief Toxicologist*

OPINION	
Time of Death	*Cold water immersion prevents TOD analysis based on body temperature or post-rigor/livor mortis. Best approximation 12:00 AM to 11:59 PM 12/25/2017.*
Immediate Cause of Death	*Drowning*
Remarks	*None*
Affirmed by	*Gregory Arnold, MD* *12/28/2017 1:57 PM*

In Loving Memory
Evan Michael Shipman

Dr. Evan Michael Shipman of Crozet, professor of U.S. History at the University of Virginia, Captain in the U.S. Army Reserve, visiting lecturer at Georgetown University, author, beloved husband and father, died by drowning Saturday, December 25, 2017, at age 43.

Evan was born in Fayetteville, North Carolina on October 11, 1974, to U.S. Army Lieutenant Harold Dean Shipman and Suzanne Gaines Shipman. Tragically, Evan never met his father, who was killed in a plane crash in Laos in 1974.

Evan graduated from Summit High School in Brevard, North Carolina. Growing up, Evan played high school basketball, ran track, and was captain of the Summit cross country team that won the 1992 Class 2 state championship.

Evan earned an athletic scholarship to George Washington University, where he received a Bachelor of Science degree in Economics. After three years in the US Army, he worked on Capitol Hill for US Senator James K. Warner of Connecticut. At age 28, Evan pursued a doctorate in US History at UVA. In 2004, he was recalled to active military duty and served two tours of duty as an infantry officer in the Iraq war.

Evan was a gifted teacher with a unique gift for bringing history to life for his students. An avid explorer, he traveled to more than 40 countries; he often said his top three were Israel, Russia, and New Zealand. On many Saturdays he could be found building houses with Habitat for Humanity of DC. A lover of music, Evan taught himself the piano, and he once donated $500 to the UVA Symphony Orchestra so he could conduct "Sleigh Ride" at the annual Christmas concert.

Though Evan and his beloved late wife Natalie Colby Shipman were both reared in Transylvania County in western North Carolina, they never met until years later on the Metro train in Washington D.C. A whirlwind romance quickly ensued, and a year later they were married. Their bliss was multiplied when Natalie gave birth to their baby girl Shelby Harper Shipman, named after Evan's favorite historian Shelby Foote and Natalie's favorite author Harper Lee. A special needs child, Shelby brought joy and love into every day, as well as a slower, more thoughtful pace to their lives. Natalie and Shelby died in 2016.

Evan is preceded in death by his mother and father, his beloved wife and daughter, and his older brother Andrew, who died at the age of five. He is survived by his stepfather James "Spud" Ellison and half-sister, Robin Ellison Miles, both of Brevard, North Carolina.

Funeral ceremonies will be Saturday December 30 at Bradshaw Funeral Care in Crozet, Virginia. Pallbearers are Dr. Jacob Martinson, Dr. Robert Ellison, John Banks, Gabriel Banks, and David R. Miles. In lieu of flowers, please consider memorial donations to the National Downs Syndrome Society at www.ndss.org.

McLean Psychiatrist Questioned in Death of UVA Professor

By Claudia Snow

December 30, 2017

MCLEAN—A Fairfax County psychiatrist was questioned by police Friday regarding the death of a University of Virginia professor.

Dr. Jacob Martinson, 44, of McLean was reportedly interviewed by Albemarle Sheriff Jim Stocker related to the drowning death of Dr. Evan M. Shipman, 43, a U.S. history professor at UVA.

Shipman's frozen body was discovered in the ice of a lake near his home in Crozet on December 26 by several youths who live in the area.

According to multiple sources, Martinson treated Shipman for insomnia and depression following the deaths of his wife and daughter, who drowned in the same lake exactly one year before Shipman's death.

Shipman and Martinson were reportedly friends since college at George Washington University, raising ethical concerns and accusations of malpractice. State medical codes discourage psychiatric treatment of family and close friends.

"We are wondering about the judgment of this so-called therapist," says Robin Miles, Shipman's half-sister. "It's obviously a conflict of interest to treat someone who's been a friend for many years."

Shipman's drowning death was initially thought accidental, but further investigation has led to questions about Shipman's state of mind and whether the incident may have been an intentional suicide.

On the last day of the year, two boys stand on the shore of the frozen lake, throwing rocks and watching them bounce across the ice.

"I'm gonna be in big trouble if my mama catches me down here," the younger boy says.

"Just keep your damned mouth shut and she won't never know," says the older boy.

The younger boys stops throwing rocks and stares out across the ice. "Do you think the lake is haunted now?"

"Haunted?" The older boy laughs.

"Three people drowned here. They say Dr. Shipman drowned himself on purpose."

"Aw, hell. Why would he do that?"

"Maybe because he missed his wife and his little girl."

"Bullshit." The older boy throws a rock. "Nobody could miss that little freak. Remember how she was? He probably killed 'em hisself to get a minute of peace."

"You shouldn't talk like that."

"Aw, hell. I knew old Shitman was crazy that day he came after us with that axe."

The younger boy turns and frowns. "I said don't talk like that. He probably saved your life that day."

"Shut up."

The talk ends. The boys hike up the hill then split up, each toward his own home.

As the sun sets over the woods, a trio of white-tailed deer stand silently on the hillside. A breeze sweeps across the meadow, blowing snow like dry dust across the frozen lake. As the last light fades, the deer turn and flee, floating across the field and vanishing into the woods with the grace of ghosts.

CONTRIBUTORS

Virginia Watson is a medical technical writer and instructional designer, specializing in the field of public health. While she normally has to stay firmly rooted in the non-fiction realm, she develops narrative case studies and other fictionalized scenarios to enhance and magnify learning at every opportunity.

I chose the month of January with no expectations or ideas about the story that would evolve. A quick dive into the etymology of the word introduced me to the Roman god Janus, about whom I knew very little. The more I studied his mythology and why the month of January is named for him, the more fascinated, but also saddened, I became. He is the god of doorways, gates, transitions – coming or going, but never just "there" – and his two faces are forever looking back at the old year and simultaneously forward to the new year, but he never gets to just "be" in the moment. I began to feel very heavy, as if the weight of Janus' responsibility was sitting on my chest. And I wondered...If it's that onerous to me, how must he feel? How would someone, who for centuries has been so plodding and dependable and who has become quite apathetic, ever work up the courage to make a break for it? In the end, he has to face an even more courageous decision: will he escape, or will he decide to engage with the world as it is?

Benjamin Carr is a writer, storyteller and editor in Atlanta. His work has appeared in The Guardian, The Five Hundred and Pembroke Magazine. His work has also been featured at The Moth Atlanta, The North Avenue Lounge, Write Club Atlanta, Carapace and The Center for Puppetry Arts.

I puzzled over my month for a good long while before deciding what about it would be interesting. Instead of finding a detail about February and exploiting it, I instead made a list of all the cliches that I didn't want to write. I didn't want to write directly about Valentine's Day or Black History Month or Leap Year. I didn't want my story to turn into some Garry Marshall romantic comedy trope. So I made a list of words that described the month, and my characters and genre kind of sprung from that. You'll find bits and pieces of February sprinkled throughout it if you look really hard. (Hilariously, it takes place in July.)

....

Samantha Thomson LoCoco earned her Master of Fine Arts degree from The New School's Creative Writing program with a concentration in fiction. While in the program, she worked as a Creative Writing Fellow, Teaching Assistant, and editor, honing her skills as a dedicated advocate for exceptional writing. Originally from Dallas, Samantha now lives in Inwood with her husband and two dogs. She writes poetry, non-fiction, and fiction, and is currently at work on her first novel.

In New York, the month of March encompasses tragically beautiful dichotomies. While the remnants of brutal winters linger, if you look closely, the budding promise of green peeks through the patina of sodden, brown muck leftover by the heavy weight of snow. Life and death sharing the same landscape. People lose a layer or two in March. You might be able to go without a hat or a scarf. You might leave a button undone on your heavy winter coat to let the not-so-affrontingly cold air touch your skin, reminding yourself it's a relationship to nature you once welcomed before the skies turned so gray and unkind.

This duality and sense of lightening brought to mind a decades-long relationship, a marriage of equal partners seeing the world differently. Thus, Mildred and Willis Sycamore Oliphant were born. This story reflects how a relationship resonates even after its physical end much like those stubborn blades of grass that push their way up through the dead leaves every spring. There can be new life in death, and new love at the end of a marriage.

....

Sara Van Beckum is a writer and actor living in Portland, Oregon. As a Meisner-trained actor, Sara was a founding member of NYC's InViolet Theater. It was in a playwriting class with Stephen Adly Guirgis where she first found her voice as a writer.

Sara makes her living doing voiceovers out of her home studio and has recorded hundreds of commercials for TV and radio. When she's not telling stories about products like mouthwash, body lotion, or dog food, she spends time inventing her own.

Sara is currently working on a novel and a collection of short stories.

Twitter: @saravanb

I selected April which marks the beginning of my own personal new year since my birthday falls on the first of the month. This story came to me in the form of a tiny, reticent bud one spring ago.

....

Meg Cassidy is an Assistant Director at Fortier Public Relations, a firm specializing in author publicity and book marketing. She has held senior-level roles at Tin House Books and Simon & Schuster, where she led campaigns for many of the imprint's lead business and lifestyle titles. Among the many bestselling and noted authors Meg has worked with are Richard Dawkins, Howard G. Buffett, Joy Williams,

Dominique Ansel, James Lee Burke, and Ruth Wariner. Meg graduated summa cum laude with degrees in English Writing and Women's Studies from Saint Mary's College in Notre Dame, IN. A Teach For America alumna, she currently volunteers with Girls Write Now, a creative-writing mentoring program for high school girls who are talented emerging authors, and edits their annual anthology.

Twitter: cassideem

Instagram: mcassidy9

Springtime and adolescence have an obvious correlation, but in this story I wanted to explore how the "late spring" season in a young woman's life has expanded so dramatically over the past few decades. Growing up in rural Wisconsin, my friends' older sisters always appeared so wise and settled—when in reality they were probably in their early 20s. But the expectation for many in that area was still to stay local, marry young, and settle into a life of motherhood. Late May, when spring leaves are reaching full maturity, can represent the end of innocence, but it shouldn't have to mean the end of growing—as it's also the season when other things are just beginning to ripen.

....

Myke Johns is a public radio producer in Atlanta, Georgia, where he covers arts and culture. His work has earned awards from the Georgia Association of Broadcasters and the Associated Press. He is a co-host of WRITE CLUB, a live literary series which kicks the ass of most any poetry reading you'd care to name. His work has appeared in The Bitter Southerner, Creative Loafing Atlanta, The Tusk, Used Gravitrons, and the anthology Bare-Knuckled Lit. He records music as Meaning of Everything.

For fart jokes and anger, his Twitter handle is @Mykayak

June is generally a joyful, celebratory month for me, full of anniversaries, birthdays, and occasions that fill life with meaning. So "209" began from those twin ideas: How do we experience joy and what does it mean to be alive? From there, it was a short, strange hop, skip and jump to imbuing a house with those questions and here we are.

....

Richard Etchison is a playwright, screenwriter, and public relations pro based in New York City. Richard's stage plays have been produced or workshopped in New York City, Los Angeles, Atlanta, Greenville, SC, Dayton, OH and Muncie, IN. He is deep in revisions on his first novel, a coming-of-age story called The Haven. Richard is a founding member of InViolet Theater Company in New York. Orphaned at a young age, he was raised by his half-sister in Florida, and graduated from the Florida State University's Creative Writing Program. He is grateful every day to be married to the public relations executive Debbie Etchison.

I have been writing for 30 years, and this story was my most autobiographical. I wanted to portray, from the point of view of a child, the most important turning point of his life. For me, the memories are extremely hazy. From a nine-year-old's point of view, such serious life changes are unfathomable. A boy stays in the moment, the glory of childhood. These three points informed my premise for the story, trying to capture the delicate innocence of a child with only a morsel of awareness that he is about to go through something difficult. My father and I traveled the country every summer after my mother died (when I was five), and then he died in 1979.

Tallie Gabriel is an artist based in Brooklyn, New York. She primarily writes young adult fiction and is endlessly grateful for the support she receives from her agent at Stonesong Literary. When not writing, Tallie is an actor and cellist and leaves the country as often as possible. She's a member of InViolet Theater Company and most recently had the pleasure of acting in the premiere of fellow company member Lia Romeo's "What Happened That Night." She plays in the indie folk duo Drunk June and is constantly harassing her friends to attend jam sessions. talliegabriel.com

My dad, his two siblings, and their father were all born in two-day increments in August. Growing up, that month always felt magical to me, especially when we'd spend it at my grandfather's house in Santa Fe. August also brought the most incredible twilights and desert rains to my hometown of Las Vegas. I never minded that it was the end of summer—rather, I loved the feeling that summer had fully set in, grown into itself. Even though Augusts in New York are humid and smell like garbage, I'm lucky enough to live near the water where they still feel endless and perfect.

As many people are, I'm fascinated by the idea of what happens to us after we die. I'm not sure what I believe, but I wanted to give myself the thought experiment of imagining what a Heaven scenario might look like. For me, Heaven would be perpetual August, and so it was with Jake. I chose to deal with a young death for a couple of reasons: The first being that I usually write from a teenage perspective, so Jake is honestly on the older side for me, and the second that I experienced the too-young death of a boyfriend's brother when I was in high school, and have never fully stopped trying to reconcile with the concept of someone who should have had so much life left losing it so quickly

Jennifer Bowen's plays include the solo show Burning Down to Heaven about the poet Anne Sexton (The Marsh Theater and Venue 9 in San Francisco; Women's Center Stage/Culture Project in NYC), full length plays Happiest Place on Earth (The Lark, Workshop/Reading InViolet Theater Company 2012, Trustus Playwrights Festival Finalist 2012), The Little Prince$$ (Workshop Production InViolet Theater Company 2014), and Ruin (Kitchen Dog Theater Finalist 2014, Trustus Playwrights Festival Finalist 2014).

Jennifer is a proud member of the InViolet Theater Company. Her films include the independently produced full length Sad Sack Sally and the short films The Silent Treatment (48 Hour Philadelphia Film Festival 2012 winner), and I (Eggs) You (Designer Vision/48 Hour Film Project Invitational). After her first stab at Young Adult Fiction, she yearned for feedback from teenage readers, and the idea for her company BookHive Corp., an organized beta reader process, was born. BookHive was selected to attend Startup Alley at the Book Expo of America in 2015 as "One of Twenty Startups to Watch." She is currently writing her first Literary Fiction Novel My Grief is Golden and True. Jennifer is a graduate of NYU Tisch School of the Arts and lives in New York with her husband and daughter.

My month was September and I liked that it was a transitional seasonal month. Whether my title character Stevens likes it or not, time does pass, seasons do change, and that is one of the driving themes of the story. The spark for creating the world of *In the Cool* began when I watched Park Chan-wook's film 'Stoker.' I was inspired by its exploration of subverted expectations of traditional family dynamics and the power of suspenseful violence. Not traditional violence, but a kind of emotional violence we do to ourselves and others when not living in awareness.

Michael Owl is the pen name for Michael Henry Harris. Michael's grandfather, Henry Owl, changed his last name in an attempt to reduce the discrimination his children would face. Michael reclaims the name with the hope his grandfather's fears will soon be unfounded.

Michael is a writer, actor, podcaster, Founding Co-Artistic Director of InViolet Theater company and Head Turkey at Pinecone Turkey. His fiction has appeared in Tender Bloodsport Volume One and Deer Bear Wolf Magazine Issue #4. He is currently working on his first novel. For more information visit pineconeturkey.com.

October is a beauty queen of a month to be sure. It's my favorite (earmuffs, December) and the favorite of many others too, including writers. When I picked this month, I imagined I'd be writing something that captured my love of Fall, something nostalgic and mysterious. I pictured Ray Bradbury and Neil Gaiman reading my story by the first fire of the year, sipping hot cider or whiskey, nodding to themselves, "now *that's* October."

The results are quite different. It took me many months and several false starts before deciding that a good ol' fashion horror story was the way to go. And then one afternoon I watched the tall trees in our yard sway during a storm. I wondered how many storms like this they'd seen. That made me wonder what else they'd borne witness to.

Virginia Underwood is a sometimes writer, sometimes attorney living and working in Atlanta, Georgia.
Website: thebeautyskewl.com

November always evokes Thanksgiving for me, as it probably does for most Americans. It's a holiday that is full of contradictions, for a day we all set aside the knowledge of our country's violent history and pretend everything went smoothly. It's also a holiday where many of us attend obligatory family dinners and put up with relatives we usually avoid. In the midst of celebrating unity, we are faced with the knowledge that division lies under the surface, and that some contradictions cannot be reconciled. Often we're tempted to pretend this turmoil does not exist. But strength comes from embracing flaws, and putting aside ideals of perfection. When we stop trying to force our lives, and the people in them, to fit a false narrative, we can be freed from the false narrative that we've written for ourselves

....

Steven Sanders has worked as a news writer in Kentucky, a bartender in Alabama, and a bike messenger in Manhattan – the toughest job he ever had. He has failed at learning to surf on numerous occasions in both the Atlantic and Pacific Oceans. He once canoed the Churchill River over 700 miles through the wilderness of northern Canada, getting into several skirmishes with bears along the way. He is the former co-founder and managing editor of SOAR Magazine and SOAR Online, a bi-monthly publication exploring outdoor adventure and recreation in the southern Appalachians. For the past decade, he has slugged it out in the world of corporate compliance and risk management. He currently lives with his wonderful wife Terese and their two mutts in Stone Mountain, Georgia. His future plans include riding a motorcycle across America, completing a tour of the Kentucky Bourbon Trail, and publishing his first novel, War Wolves.

Late on a December night after everyone was asleep, I was sitting alone in the dark sipping a good bourbon and listening to a slow jazz song about a man skating on a frozen pond. My mind was hypnotized by the drifting saxophone solo and the wire brushes dragging across the snare drum like skate blades hissing over the ice. I had been reading about the ancient habit of segmented sleep—going to bed at sunset, rising for a few hours in the middle of the night, then sleeping again until dawn—and how the mind is especially calm and lucid during the waking interval. A few weeks later my wife was out of town for several days, and I experimented with this segmented sleep pattern, going to bed at sundown and rising on the far side of midnight to write this story by candlelight, that sad saxophone solo and rhythmic snare still drifting through my mind.

ACKNOWLEDGEMENTS

This book would not exist without the efforts of several talented people.

The first being, of course, the writers. Thank you for taking this leap with me and creating something new. Thank you for your patience as I learn on the job.

Thanks to Adam Robinson for being my publishing coach, cheerleader, and all around person who knows things.

Thanks to my co-editor and contributor Samantha Thomson LoCoco for raising my game, and that of the authors she worked with. This collection is so much better for her insight, talent, and hard work. She has gifts.

Thanks to Peggy and Hank for their love and support.

Thanks to my Mom and all her encouragement and wisdom. I love you, Mom. I miss you, Mom.

THANK YOU FOR SUPPORTING
INDEPENDENT PUBLISHING.

KEEP UP WITH EVERYTHING
PINECONE TURKEY.

JOIN PINECONE TURKEY'S EMAIL LIST
THE FLOCK!

TWO EMAILS A MONTH.
ONE CONTAINS YOUR MINIMUM MONTHLY
DOSE OF ART,

THE OTHER THE LATEST NEWS ABOUT ALL
THINGS PINECONE TURKEY INCLUDING:

THE OWLS ON CULTURE PODCAST
*Two generations of Owls, Michael the Dad (46 yrs old) and Hank
the Son (12 yrs old,) discuss the latest in movies, t.v. shows, video
games, books, and more.*

THE ORIGIN STORY PODCAST
*It's my favorite part of every superhero story, it's the Origin Story,
and we all have one.*

*Join Michael Henry Harris in long-form conversations with
superheros from all walks of life.*

AND NEWS ABOUT OUR UPCOMING RELEASE

12 AUTHORS 12 STORIES 2019

Sign up for The Flock at
http://pineconeturkey.com/

Made in the USA
Columbia, SC
19 December 2018